Tales from Tiger Bay

Other Books by Alexander Cordell:

Rape of the Fair Country.
The Hosts of Rebecca.
Song of the Earth.
A Thought of Honour.
The Fire People.
Race of the Tiger.
To Slay the Dreamer.
The Enemy Within.
If You Believe The Soldiers.
The Sinews of Love.
The Bright Cantonese.
The Dream and the Destiny.
This Sweet and Bitter Earth.
Rogue's March.
Land of my Fathers.
Peerless Jim.
Tunnel Tigers.

BOOKS FOR CHILDREN
Sea Urchin.
The White Cockade.
Witch's Sabbath.
The Healing Blade.
The Traitor Within.

TALES FROM TIGER BAY

A Collection of Short Stories

by

Alexander Cordell

BLORENGE BOOKS

First published in Great Britain 1986 by Blorenge Books

ISBN 0 9510444 3 5

•

The characters and situations in this book are
entirely imaginary and bear no relation to any real person
(excepting the landlord of the *Duke of Edinburgh*)
or actual happening

•

BLORENGE BOOKS
3, Holywell Road, Abergavenny, Gwent, NP7 5LP
Tel: Abergavenny 3909

Printed by Adams & Sons (Printers) Ltd., Hereford

For Kit and Michael Flynn of

the Royal Oak Hotel, Cardiff,

relatives of the immortal

Peerless Jim.

Acknowledgements

The author is grateful to the B.B.C. for permission to reproduce here the stories *Eastern Promise, Divine Intervention, Fragrant Concubines, Adam's Sin* and *Caesar's Wife* (broadcast on Radio Four); also to *The Western Mail* for permission to reproduce the stories *Obituary, O'Brien's Christmas Ghost, The Last Bare-knuckle, The Phantom Match* and *The Widow of Kildare.*

Contents

The sequence of events are not necessarily in order.

Introduction

What is there, I wonder, that makes a beloved place linger in the heart? The answer is this — it's the people. And the people who inhabited Tiger Bay have engraved their personalities on the very air of Bute Street.

The older among us remember, of course, when Irish fiddles were singing along Pendoylan and squeeze boxes blasted and there was dancing in the snugs. Sophia, North William Street and Ellen Street! The *Cape Horn* and the *Blood Kitchen* where Jim Driscoll sparred: does his ghost walk up Ellen Street hand in hand with Edie Wiltshire?

Home of the extravagant rich and the pallid poor. *Tiger Bay!* The name conjours its own brand of magic; the Port that threw open its arms to the world and bred a City. Dead? Not on your life. As grandmother to all its colourful past in memory, Tiger Bay is still vividly and gloriously alive.

Alexander Cordell

The Widow of Kildare

'... there arrived from Kildare about then a shy, sweet widow called Beth O'Shea, and Joby took one look at her and smoke came out of his ears.'

• 1 •

The Widow of Kildare

Father O'Brien's the name, and I used to be the parish Priest down on Cardiff's Dockland, ye know. There were about twenty pubs in Newtown at the turn of the century, and I knew every one, for you try being a teetotaller in an Irish town in Wales.

Indeed, the only true teetotaller I ever came across was Joby Sarsaparilla, who humped the flour bags on Atlantic Wharf: he sank a quart of it every night in *The Duke of Edinburgh*, Jim Driscoll's pub — the landlord got it in especially.

A single man was Joby, and the women put years on themselves at the sight of him, smoothing down their hips and pushing up their busts, but he never spared them a glance: for there arrived from Kildare about then a shy, sweet widow called Beth O'Shea, and Joby took one look at her and smoke came out of his ears.

I was relieved at this, for if there's anything likely to cause a commotion, it's a stag in rut, and marital business claimed me special attention.

They were suited those two — Joby and Beth — for rumour had it that her first chap had drunk himself to death, so she was a'feared of anything to do wi' hops and barmaid's aprons.

"D'ye think he's the man for me, holy Father?" she asked me one day after confessional.

"Ach, sure," said I. "He's a sarsaparilla man, isn't he? After your first bad experience, what more do ye want?" And we stood there together in the sea wind and sun, and I knew a stirring in my heart I'd never felt before. "I'll personally guarantee your happiness, sweet child," I said to her, and she bowed to me and went off with a pretty swing of the hips.

She was a darling, delicate girl, and she turned once and waved to me, but I could not wave back. Never had I taken a shine to a woman till then, and I said to myself, "Treat her wrong, Joby Sarsaparilla, and I'll see to ye, as God's me judge."

Well, I married 'em in St. Paul's, and it was like a crucifixion, having to part with her, and a month later I was in *The Duke of Edinburgh* and Jim Driscoll himself was drawing me a quart o' Guinness from the wood, which I took for medicinal purposes.

And who should be sitting at a table in there but Joby, with a glass of sarsaparilla in front of him and grinning like a Cheshire cat.

"How's ye doing, son? Is she treating you well?" I asked him.

"Aye, foine, foine, Father," says he. "She boils the best Irish stew between here and Kildare, so she does, and I'm away home to her now," and the moment he'd gone I realised he'd drunk me quart of Guinness and left me his quart of sarsaparilla.

"What happened to that?" I asked Jim, holding up me pewter. "Did he drink it or did it evaporate?"

Sober serious was the boxer — he rarely touched a drop. "Father," said he, "the devils of Gehenna are roamin' in a man who doesn't know the difference between Guinness and sarsaparilla."

"Ye can say that again," said I.

The devils were in young Joby after that, and I blamed meself for it, I did — putting strong drink in his path like that. Aye, the chap went from bad to worse once he'd got the taste for it — night after night he rode home on the back of a pig to that wee girl — and when I met her in Ellen Street one day with an eye filled up, I decided to take a hand in their matrimonial affairs.

Mind, I could have mentioned it to Jim — he was right handy with drunks who gave black eyes to wives — but I didn't: I didn't because within the hour I saw Joby staggering out of the *Erin go bragh* tavern with scarcely a leg beneath him, so I politely escorted him through the dark to his home; holding him up, I heaved him into the kitchen, and my wee Beth saw him, and sighed: she sighed, I say, as a man sighs when nails go through his hands.

"Where d'ye want him, girl?"

"On the bed upstairs, if you please," and in the half light from the street I saw her tears.

I did a fireman's lift up the stairs and flung him on to the bed, and he lay on his back with snores comin' from his belted belly more like a hog than a man.

We stood together, her and me, and I said, holding her hands:

"Beth, this has got to change, ye know?"

"Aye, Father, aye. Now leave us. What I have to do I must do alone."

So I left her with him and went down the stairs, but, impelled by a sudden fear, I stopped and looked through the banisters into the room.

First, Beth sat on the bed beside him; taking off her shoes, she pulled up her dress and unfastened her stockings; these she draped over the bedrail — one at the head of the bed, one at the bottom. Then she knelt as if in prayer for a few seconds, and rose.

With one stocking she tied Joby's feet to the bottom rail; with the other stocking she tied his hands to the top rail of the bed. Climbing on to the bed she then straddled his chest, as one rides a horse, and taking from her pocket a half bottle of whisky, she said at the ceiling:

"Dear God, forgive me, but what can I do?" and she added pulling out the cork, "Have this on me, Joby Sarsaparilla," and she opened his mouth and poured in the whisky, slammed his mouth shut and leaned upon his face.

Joby leaped on the bed like a bucking broncho. Gulping, gurgling, he arched his body and nearly threw her off, but she hung on. He was bawling now, but she got her forearm across his face and held his nose and poured in more. After a bit he subsided, did Joby, for three quarts o' Guinness and half-a-bottle of rye would put to sleep the toss-pots of Jerusalem.

Still astride him, but with her hands over her face, she wept.

He missed six shifts on the Atlantic Wharf, did Joby. They heard him splutterin' all the way up North William Street.

Being pay day, I was in *The Duke of Edinburgh* a fortnight later, and I'd just got me teeth into my complimentary Guinness when in comes young Joby. Very pale around the gills he was and walking on tin-tacks.

"A quart o' Guinness, Mr. Driscoll," says he. "It's a hair o' the bitch that bit me, in a manner of speaking."

"Have ye been off colour, then, you poor soul?" I asked.

"I have, holy Father. Ye see, I chased the Guinness with neat rye — six pints and half-a-bottle — and it upset me somethin' terrible, so it did."

"Aye, that's a dangerous thing to do, lad," said Jim Driscoll. "Do you recall that fella up in Kildare doing it, Father, and he died?"

"I do. That was terrible sad," said I, and I took Joby's quart from Jim and passed it on to the table.

"What happened, then?" asked Joby lifting his pewter.

I replied. "Well, this big oaf, he kept getting himself plastered and comin' home to his missus wi' his back teeth awash, see? She was a dear, sweet girl, but she got sick of it, with no money in the house and him blacking her eyes. So, one night she tied him to the bed-posts, and filled him up with whisky."

"Mark, Mary and Joseph!" ejaculated Joby, and jumped, and he got more Guinness down the front of him than into his mouth. "Kildare, did ye say, for God's sake?"

"Aye. The Widow of Kildare, they called her in the newspapers. But she's living round these parts somewhere now, they tell me."

Very delicate looked Joby.

"Mind you," explained Jim, "she didn't mean to harm him,

only cure him ..."

"Which is why she got away with it at the inquest," said I.

"Well, sod me," said Joby.

"Watch your language in front of the holy Father!" interjected Jim.

Joby got up. With one hand over his mouth and the other on the door, very shaky he looked. "Draw me a glass o' sarsaparilla, for God's sake," cried he, "for I'm finished wi' that filthy brew," and the moment he was through the door I sank his Guinness.

"Which is right and fair," said Jim, "for he owed you a quart. But ..." and he put out his hand. "But you still owe me for that half-a-bottle of whisky."

• • •

Heavenly Correspondent

‘Even the mice were listening as I read:

“*To God, care of New Way Temperance Society.*” ’

• 2 •

Heavenly Correspondent

Long ago, when I was its parish Priest, things were hard for the children of our town. And when Christmas came around, times got harder; no Christmas trees, little to eat, no fun. With this in mind I applied for the assistance of the New Way Temperance Society; the chairman of their committee was the local postmaster, and I didn't find him wanting.

"The good Lord will pour blessing on your generous souls," said I, and I was wiping whiskers and stepping out of the *Duke of Edinburgh* when I saw this fella coming.

"Have ye been in that den of ale-swilling iniquity, holy Father?" asked he, astonished.

"I have," said I. "I've been lecturing the customers in there on the evils of strong drink, for it's the children of the neighbourhood who suffer, and they're first and last with me."

"Pleased I am to hear it," replied he, "for the wee mites have set us a problem. One has just written a letter to God."

I got windward of the fella so he couldn't smell me breath. "You mean, one of the parish kids has addressed a letter to Heaven, and you've got it?"

"That's it, Father O'Brien," said the Postmaster. "Every year we get dozens addressed to Father Christmas, of course, but how d'ye ignore a request to the Almighty?"

"You don't, son. You comply with it. What does the letter say?"

"Good grief!" cried he, and shook like a jelly. "Would I tempt official wrath by opening God's private correspondence? But since it's been sent care of the Temperance Society and you're a priest, perhaps you'd consider opening and reading it at tomorrow's Annual General Meeting?"

"In me official capacity as the Pope's representative ye mean?"

"May the saints bless ye, Holy Father," said he.

"Are all the members present and attentive?" cried the Postmaster next evening in the local hall. "For we've had a communication from a child of simple faith to God, and Father O'Brien's about to open the envelope and read the letter."

Even the mice were listening as I read:

'To God, care of New Way Temperance Society.
Dear God,
Me name's Susie Murphy, I live in Six Tyndall. Me father died of drink, me ma's on the gin, and me gran's crying her eyes out because she can't pay the rent. We'll be out in the street for sure come Christmas.
Please God, could you send me three pounds? Two pounds for our gran, so she can pay the rent, and a pound for me to spend on Bridget, Maire, Bella, Sam, Alby, Joe, Carys and Tam. I'm not wanting anything for myself.
Love,
Susie Murphy.'

Now, before I was half-way through that letter, all present were sniffing and wiping: the borough treasurer was sobbing on the shoulder of the mayor, the county slaughterer crying like a child. Indeed, I was so full that I had to pull meself together; and I went round with the hat before they could take another breath.

"Two pounds eight shillings!" cried the Postmaster, counting it, and he dropped in a couple of bob to make it up to two-pounds-ten," and rose, crying:

"Gentlemen, gentlemen, a most excellent collection! Thank you, thank you! The money will be sent to wee Susie Murphy in the name of God."

A few days after Christmas, I was on my way into the *Erin go Bragh* tavern for a wee drop when I saw the Postmaster coming again, so I stopped to tie up me bootlaces.

"We've got another letter addressed to God," said he. "Look, it's the same handwriting. It'll be from that sweet Susie Murphy of Tyndall Street."

"Without a doubt," said I.

"And since tonight there's a special meeting to consider the destruction of all alcoholic beverages, I suggest you do the same as before — open it and read it from the top table."

"It'll be a pleasure."

This was a crowded meeting, called especially for the tipping of a barrel of Allsops down the drain, all members present, which didn't upset me overmuch since I'm more partial to whisky chasers.

"Ladies and gentlemen," cried the Postmaster. "Father O'Brien has kindly agreed to open another letter addressed to the Deity — without a doubt it's from that dear child Susie Murphy, to whom we sent the money," and I opened the envelope and read:

'Dear God,

Thank you for your letter enclosing two-pounds-ten, but don't you remember, I asked you for three pounds? In future, when I ask for money, don't send it through those thieving sods of the New Way Temperance Society.'

• • •

•

Now, I've told you a couple of tall ones and you've weighed me up by now; and you're probably wondering who this O'Brien fella is for he's chock full o' the blarney for a Priest in Holy Orders. And, come to think of it, there's no good reason why you should have heard of me at all.

But whatever you think of these yarns, I'm telling you one thing — every word of what I write is true — as true as life, if I never move from here.

•

The Prince of Darkness

'I could see footprints in the snow that led down to the road; the shape of them took my eye, and I pulled my dressing-gown closer about me and went out into the night.

'Bending, I peered down.

'They were the imprints, not of a human shoe, but of a cloven hoof.'

• 3 •

The Prince of Darkness

There's no good reason why you should have heard of me. You could ask in Ireland from Donegal to Kerry and you'd come across a hundred or so Father Sean O'Briens. But, were you to inquire in Cardiff, you'd likely be referring to Tiger Bay — the Dockland — for this is me stamping ground. And the next thing you'd hear is that I tell a good yarn and that what I don't know I make up. Aye, well I admit to a wee bit of the blarney, but I tell you this — when I talk of my conversations with the Deity, every word is true: true, I'm tellin' you — on a baby's life.

Now, me marvellous affinity with *The Man in the Big Pew* (as the Baptists call Him) didn't come after I became Father Sean O'Brien, oh dear no! It occurred first when I was a stripling of a chap, lusty and eager, one hot afternoon in July long before I dreamed of taking the Cloth. Aye, it happened when I was walking barefooted on the sands of Ballacroy with the finest-looking piece of crumpet this side of Connemara: I had me arm around the waist of the marvellous creature, weighing up the pros and cons of getting her horizontal (I had brought a picnic tea) when I heard God's voice, and so did she.

"Are ye there, Sean O'Brien?" asked God.

"Providence and mercy spare us!" exclaimed she. "Did you hear that?"

"I heard nothing," said I.

"As sure as me name's Bridget O'Callaghan, I heard a fella call your name!" and she bummed up her skirts and went like a hare coursing up the beach.

"Well, that's one way to get rid of them," said God. "Are ye listening, O'Brien?"

"That I am, Your Worship," said I, and I was shivering to lay me bones out.

"Then pay attention," replied God.

And I felt like Moses must have done when he heard God's voice from the midst of the burning bush.

The sun burned down. Up in the blue a lark was singing, I remember, his voice a cadence on the sultry air.

God said, "Have you ever thought of taking the Cloth, O'Brien? Becoming one of me shepherds, and all that?"

"I have not," I replied, when I'd found me tongue. "For I'm a wicked chap six days of the week and depend on the Confessional on Sundays." I added, "And I'm not worthy to wear the sacred habit of a priest."

"Aha!" exclaimed God. "The first quality — humility. Fine, fine! Now, do ye think you could handle the intellectual necessities of a clerical life?"

"Ach no, Your Honour, I'm as daft as a brush."

"Most of them are, so no odds to that," said God. "And I can see that you're sincere and genuine, since I'm getting the most honest replies. Humility, Sincerity and Simplicity — that's what I'm looking for in a priest — consider yourself ordained."

"But I'd never pass the examinations!"

"I'll have a word to the Principal, so don't worry on that score. There's only one aspect of your character that's bothering me now, my son, and that's your relationship with women. Reading your mind a few minutes ago, I found there's much to be desired. Have another go at it O'Brien, I'll bring the woman back."

And bless me soul to hell, I look up and there was Bridget O'Callaghan coming back down the beach to me, and she sidled up to me like Delilah must have done before Samson lost his eyesight, sat down on the sand and patted it for me to join her. "Sure, ye darlin' thing," said she, "I must have been hearing things, for I guess it was only the wind," and her face was fair and her eyes were blue and I didn't know if I was on me ear or me elbow, but I got away a yard and said to her:

"Bridget O'Callaghan, you're a scarlet woman, and I'm havin' nothing to do wi' ye, so away sharp before I get me rag out," and she went.

"Well done," said God. "Years back I lined up another fella for the same sort of thing and he didn't do so good — his name was Adam."

And God took my hand and led me, and my step was so light I scarcely touched the sand.

Well, to cut a long yarn short, I was standing on the steps of Dublin cathedral wearing the habit of a priest five years later when a voice whispered into my ear:

"I'm considering your first living, Father O'Brien."

It was God, and the wind blew and brought all the sounds and smells of Dublin town, including the smell of the Liffey. I stood, me ears tingling.

"Now listen," said God. "Every first appointment in the holy church is in the nature of a test for a young priest, and one of the things I find you short of is good character assessment. Like that Bridget O'Callaghan, if ye recall. You thought she was one of the seven virgins; fact is, she was a scarlet woman, and you didn't twig it."

I sighed, nodding.

"And so," continued God, "it'll be necessary to satisfy me that you've improved in that direction before I make you substantive in the post, if ye get me?"

"Yes, Sir," said I.

The people pushed about me in gesticulation and gabble; the gents in the fine morning suits, the ladies in their coloured summer dresses, and I thought it daft that I should be listening to tests about character assessment when I could have been sparking with one of a dozen young girls who were giving me the eye-and-come-hither, for their lips were red and their hair and bonnets were beautiful in the sun.

"I'd be obliged if you'd pay attention to me," said God, "for you're done wi' all that — are ye heeding me?"

I bowed my head, and he continued:

"I've got a bit of a problem coming up in Wales — and it'll prove a foine test of your understanding of the human character in all its foibles and intricacies. And if you pass wi' flying colours in that examination, the world's your oyster — do ye understand me, O'Brien?"

"Where, in Wales?" I asked. "You realise, I suppose, that I'm as Irish as you?"

"Small odds to that, O'Brien. We're all Celts under the skin, and anyway, Welshmen are only Irishmen who've never learned how to swim, so you'll be in happy company; 'tis a place called Tiger Bay, down in Cardiff's dockland."

The sun went out then, and dark clouds gathered, and I thought it was an omen. And God said, "It's a mixed community, mind. Down in the docks they've got Moslems, Hindus, Baptists and Christadelphians; Church of England, Catholic, Taoists and Buddhists, and they're every colour of the rainbow from black to yellow and chocolate brown. And, while they live happily enough together in this place called Irishtown, there's creeping in a wee bit o' pickpocketing, drunkenness, revelry and rowdiness, to say nothing of a bit of Chinese concubinage and fornication to boot, and there's some pretty long gullets hanging in places like the *Duke of Edinburgh* and the *Erin go Bragh*, and Bute Street has to be seen to be believed. Indeed, I've reason to think that His Satannic Majesty, the Incarnate Fiend is about to move in and make a killing, and this is where you come in if you pass the character assessment test I'm setting ye." God paused dramatically. "But there's something more ..."

"Tell me all," I said like a man.

"The Pope's moving in an English Bishop."

"Oh no!"

"Oh yes. As a good Irishman I naturally regret this. Ever since the slaughters of Cromwell and the hanging of Father John

Murphy I've been tryin' to get shot of the breed, but the pay's good, so they're bound to increase. And remember this, O'Brien. The Fiend can appear in many shapes and forms — he could take the mortal skin of anyone — from an Ecclesiastic Commissioner to a passing man in the street, in a pub; even an animal of cloven hoof or paw ..."

"Or an English bishop?" I asked.

"Take it as read, O'Brien. For I'm lifting out of mortal life a simple situation — one of conflict, love, insincerity and madness — and I'm tossing ye down into the middle of it and I'll watch to see what kind of a fist you make of it. Go now, and may the God you worship be generous to you, my son."

"You can say that again," said I.

Well, less than a week later I was knocking on the door of the Presbytery of St. Paul's Church, Irishtown in Tiger Bay, Cardiff, and it was opened by a witch. And if she wasn't a witch, this official housekeeper, she should have been, I thought, for she had the body of a starved ghost, a wizened face to match with a nose that curved down and a chin that curved up, and in her arms she was carrying the biggest black cat I've ever seen: give this one a broom and she'd be up and around the Irishtown chimneys, I thought; and when she spoke her voice was like a cinder under a door.

"Welcome to God's house," she croaked, and bowed, and the black cat took one look at me and spat and hissed. "Welcome, welcome, holy Father ..." and I thought she shielded her eyes from the Cross on my habit, though I could have been mistaken. "I've just been airing the bed with pans and bottles," she added, stepping aside for me to enter. "The last fella died, as you probably know. The poor dear soul, it was a happy release."

I went into the drawing-room and it had pictures of past Popes all round the walls and it was like a mausoleum, but twice as chilly. And sitting in one of the armchairs was an old fella of about eighty; sitting there as large as life was he and dressed in full rugby kit — the scarlet vest of Wales plus the three feathers, white shorts, bare boney knees, red socks and rugby boots: aye, aged eighty was he, all six foot of him, and wearing the international cap with tassle of Wales.

"My name's Martha O'Hara, Father," announced the housekeeper, wringing her hands behind me. "And this is Mr. Maldwyn Thomas Rugby.. he's a sort o' handyman around the place, if ye get me? Does all the household jobs, like sweepin' up and gettin' the coal in — while he's awaiting his call from the Welsh Selectors ..."

And she added in an undertone, "The poor soul's not quite the ticket, ye understand. He's been dressed like that for the past fifty years, but there's no blain nor wickedness in him — is there, Maldwyn — no wickedness, eh?" and Maldwyn rose to his full six feet.

"Very happy to meet you, Father O'Brien," said Maldwyn, soprano, and crushed my hand in his.

"Indeed, he's a most dependable chap, aren't you, Maldwyn? He's just been down meeting the new English bishop at Cardiff General. You knew about the English bishop arriving today as well, I suppose?"

"Don't tell me he's already here?" I was appalled.

"Ach no, settle yourself," replied Martha, flapping me down. "T'is no harm done, because the moment he telephoned for transport from the station, we organised it fine, didn't we, Maldwyn?"

"Met him in the trap and took him to the Angel Hotel," said Maldwyn. "I tell you this, holy Father, he was a right nice chap. He said he hoped you'd come to see him later, after you arrived."

"I hope you changed your clothes," I said to Maldwyn.

"Oh no, and he was delighted. For he's a rugby fanatic himself, he told me. I tell you, Father O'Brien, he's a wonderful man — six foot up and a two ton chap, and he's wearing a better pair o' cauliflower ears than Jim Driscoll over in the *Duke of Edinburgh*!"

"You seem to have handled it well, the pair of you," said I, "and I'm obliged."

Once in my bedroom, however, I said at the ceiling, "Look, did ye have to bring that new Bishop in on the day I arrived? I haven't even had me tea."

"Well," replied God, "it's the way things happen — that's life. Just take it in your stride."

"And who's this nut-case Maldwyn Thomas Rugby?" I demanded. "Isn't it enough to be landed with a witch for a housekeeper, without having a mad man pestering every living moment."

"That's how it is, and you'll have to make the best of it," anwered God. "And while I'm with you — keep an eye on that cat. For the Fiend can come in any shape or form, as I told you ..."

"Don't remind me," I said. "Good night to you, and I hope you'll treat me better in the morning."

"Forget about the morning, O'Brien. Your tribulations begin tonight. Hadn't you better stop bellyaching and get down to see your Bishop?"

So I did, first sprucing myself up and putting on my best coat.

"Shall I come with you to meet the bishop?" asked Maldwyn, in the hall.

"I'll handle this myself," said I. "You've put him in the Angel Hotel, ye say?"

"The hotel opposite the Castle walls," cried Martha from the kitchen, and I caught a tram up Bute Street.

In the reception hall of the big hotel, I said to the clerk, "Would you kindly tell his lordship, the Bishop of Llandaff, that I've arrived — Father O'Brien?"

"The Bishop of Llandaff?" The clerk, young, adenoidal, peered up at me.

"The Bishop of Llandaff?" he repeated to himself with vacant incredulity.

"That's right, that's right — the Bishop!" I said angrily.

"There ain't no Bishop staying here, Father," and he cupped his hands to his mouth, and called to a passing waiter, "Has anyone seen the Bishop of Llandaff?"

"Tell him to try Llandaff," came the answer.

"But, he must be here!" I exploded.

"One thing's sure, Sir, he ain't booked in here," said the clerk.

"Then where can he be?" I stared about me desperately.

"Search me, Sir," said the clerk, so I hailed a cab and began a hunt in Cardiff.

I eventually tracked down my Bishop in one of the lowest possible dives in Sofia Street. He was sitting in full majesty at a scrubbed table in the *Hen and Chickens*, eating faggots and peas.

Never have I seen such a man in anger. He was six feet seven, to be exact, nigh twenty stones and a foot between the eyes, and his ears were like large bits of his brain battered out of his skull. And he smiled wide and pure at me as I entered screwing my clerical hat.

"Father Sean O'Brien?" he asked, sober serious and as sweet as a nut.

"Aye, my lord, that's me," said I.

And he rose to his full height like an avenging despot, and bellowed:

"I want a word with you, O'Brien. And I want a word, too, with that ill-dressed bloody numbskull who brought me to this hovel! You realise, I suppose, that I'm a Bishop?"

"Yes, Sir!"

"Well, don't stand there saying 'Yes, sir, yes, sir' — get me out of here!"

"Yes, sir," said I, and he repeated thunderously, "GET ME OUT OF HERE!"

"You made a right cock-up of that, it would appear," said God, when I returned to the Presbytery.

"Don't remind me," said I.

"Indeed, it would appear — although the circumstances were beyond your control — that you've got off on the wrong foot with your Bishop."

I didn't reply.

"Which is unfortunate for you, to say the least, for now I intend to put your diplomacy to the test. Do well this time, O'Brien, and your future is assured, but complete failure, may I remind you, could easily affect your ultimate salvation, for Bishops have a very great influence upon confidential reports, and St. Peter puts great store on such opinions. Go carefully in the next few days."

A sudden rage seized me, and I cried, "You might have warned me that I'd be landed with that damned half-wit, Maldwyn Thomas Rugby!"

"Half-wit, did you say?" asked God. "May I tell you, O'Brien, that Maldwyn Thomas Rugby has five certificates to say he is sane, while you do not possess one. Meanwhile, as I warned you before — keep an eye on that cat. The Devil can come in the guise of a human or an animal... the cloven hoof or paw, remember ?" God added, "Now I must tell you that I'm off to China for a day or two, so do try to keep in with your Bishop until I get back."

"Please don't leave me," I begged.

"Oh, but I must. You can't expect to have advisers holding your hand in any examination, can you?" and the air moved in the room, and he was gone.

And the big black cat, I discovered later, had been listening outside the door.

Within a week of my arrival in Tiger Bay the Presbytery telephone bell rang.

"Is that you, O'Brien?" It was the Bishop's voice, double bass from Llandaff.

I froze. "Yes, your lordship."

"I require," said he, peremptorarily, "a ticket for the International rugby match between England and Wales at Cardiff Arms Park on Saturday week; please arrange it."

"But that's impossible, my lord! They're like solid gold."

"Which explains the difficulty I've been having in obtaining one. Two tickets, in fact; you can come, too, in case I need you there."

"But...!"

"Preferably in the Members' Stand," he boomed.

"But, my Lord!"

"If necessary, pray," and he was gone.

Martha moved like a black ghost of silence in the shadows of the hall. It was snowing outside, I remember; great wavering flakes drifting down on the silent Bobtail where the children played in summer: I made a mental prayer; if it snowed hard enough the International would be called off.

"Oh no," croaked Martha, coming into the lamplight, "they always 'ave the Internationals. It'll have to be six feet high down Bute before they call one off." She peered up into my face. "Tickets, he's after, is he?"

"How did you know, for God's sake?"

"My business to know, isn't it?" and she held her cat closer against her face. "Our business to know what the holy man is up to, isn't it, Baal?"

"What did you call it?"

"Baal," she repeated. "A real satan of a cat unless you understand him like me, ain't you, son? A sort o' Devil's handmaiden, but he's as right as rain when you get to know him, like I said. Tickets, is it?"

Martha scratched her ear. "You'll get those from the *Duke of Edinburgh*."

"The famous boxer? This is rugby!"

"Just ask for the tickets and Jim Driscoll will see to ye, holy father." She clutched my arm with a taloned hand. "But watch ye step, for it ain't all that easy."

"Nothing appears easy in Tiger Bay," said I.

So I hied meself over to the *Duke of Edinburgh* and over a Guinness for medicinal purposes, put the problem to Jim Driscoll, the landlord.

"There's only one fella in the whole wide world who can get you a pair of International tickets," said he, "and that's Maldwyn Thomas Rugby."

"Not him, not him!" I cried.

"Or Evan Pugh, the knife-grinder..." Jim scratched his ear.

"Spare time, he's gardener for the President of the Welsh Selectors. I've known Evan Pugh turn them up before now... he gets around, mind you, with his Billy Goat and paraffin."

"Tell him I'll see him right with God," I replied. "It's a matter of life or death," and I killed my Guinness and went out into the cold winter sunlight.

It looked like more snow, I remember thinking.

Irishtown folks huddled past me with nipped greetings, swaddled against the cold, for the wind was coming in off Tiger Bay with knives in him that winter, and the poor were having a bad time of it, and the General Strike was looming like a spectre over the land. Pale-faced women were brushing out their doorsteps and the fires were dead in their little grates within, and the bay window shops were pathetically poor, with scarcely anything to sell. But the traps and landaus were still clip-clopping down to Mount Stuart Square where the top-hatted Stock Exchange gents were buying and selling the labour they never saw; and swish-skirted ladies were being armed around by their gentry escorts: and from the blousy taverns of Sophia Street and Tyndall came the melodeon strains and bawdy choruses; the tippling drunks and boozies of the *Erin go Bragh* and *Farmers Arms*. It was a queer old world, I thought; a Bishop who wanted tickets for the International while the poor of Irishtown fiddled out their lives on pease pudding, faggots and drip.

And the wind moved from the docks and it was bitter with the tang of sulphur.

Now, it is known in the world of rugby that emotions run high when England takes on Wales at Cardiff Arms Park. The Scots and Irish are always made welcome, of course, being brother Celts; the French are tolerated although they are mainly onion-sellers, but catcalls and whistles rise from the terraces when an Englishman has to be dug out of the bottom of the ruck accompanied by remarks like, 'Let's 'ope it isn't trial,' and 'When you get him out, lads, boot 'im into touch.'

But on the day I got the tickets from Jim Driscoll on the

Saturday and escorted my gigantic bishop into the Members' Stand, the people took one look at his ears under his broad-rimmed black hat, and became ecstatic, and he returned the Welsh compliment by standing stiffly to attention while *Land of my Fathers* was done on trumpets and drums.

"O'Brien," said he portentously, sitting down, "you have done well. Indeed, I am beginning to think you can assist me greatly in the enormous plans I have for a great revival of the religious spirit in Wales."

"A revival?" And he raised blue-veined hands upwards, and cried:

"Revolutionary plans whereby the old reactionary orders shall be cast out and replaced by new and progressive ideas: down with Vatican control of Catholicism, this is my aim. Together, you and I, we could build a new Jerusalem in the very heart of Irishtown; and from this kernel could spring all the majestic ideals which I for so long have entertained. Down with the Papal hierarchy, too! I can hear a great wind of change blowing over the earth — beginning in Cardiff."

I stole a glance at my Bishop: exultation, explosive and immediate, was engraved upon his features which in that moment were contorted as if by some inner emotion, and I remembered the words of God, '... and the Fiend can appear in many forms, O'Brien... a man in the street, in a pub, even as an animal of paw or cloven hoof...' Down with the Pope? Is that what the Bishop said? Cast out the old orders and build a New Jerusalem in Irishtown?

"Good God!" I ejaculated.

"Did you say something, O'Brien?" My Bishop leaned towards me and his breath steamed in the winter frost as he confidentially pressed my knee. But in that moment a roar went up from the crowd as England kicked off, and the game was on; and in the next moment Maldwyn Thomas Rugby arrived in full rugby kit plus a six foot leek and put his rear on the vacant seat between us.

"'Afternoon, gents!"

"Oh, God Almighty!" ejaculated my Bishop. "Oh dear no, not *you!*"

"And you can cut that out," replied Maldwyn, elbowing him. "You wouldn't be 'ere, mate, if it wasn't for me, remember."

"Don't tell me he obtained the tickets!"

"He didn't!" I protested. "I got them off Evan Pugh, the knife-grinder!"

"And who gave them to Evan Pugh?" asked Maldwyn. "You think again, my lovely," and he jerked his thumb at the Bishop. "Meanwhile, you tell him that it's a mouthful of knuckles he'll be havin' if he comes the acid with me."

"Maldwyn!" I cried, shocked. "You are talking to the Bishop!"

"I don't care if he's Lloyd George's bloody father — he's been shooting off his mouth about me and the *Hen and Chickens*, and if he wants a shandibang up by 'ere he can bloody 'ave it, big as he is," and the Bishop fixed me with an icy stare, saying:

"I instructed you to obtain tickets for the match, O'Brien, but not, I may add, at the risk of personal abuse and the threat of physical violence."

Another burst of wild cheering, for the match was under way, and Wakers Wakefield had got it and was going head down for the Welsh line.

"After him, tap 'is ankle!" bawled Maldwyn, and he leaped up like a jackanape, fisting the air and bawling abuse as the Englishman was tackled by Hopkins of Swansea and brought down.

"I've got a sovereign that says we'll hit hell out of you, Pope," cried Maldwyn.

"You're on," replied the Bishop, and narrowed his eyes at me in a stoney stare.

His breath was puffing smoke in the cold air; there was upon his features a look of demoniacal fury; had he grown horns in that moment I'd have accepted him as one of the Furies from the pit of Hell.

"I will have words with you after the match, O'Brien, make no mistake upon it."

"Oh, God..." I breathed. Hearing this, the Bishop continued harshly:

"Don't call for help, O'Brien, although I think you are bound to need it. For you have made an incalculably bad impression upon me at our first two meetings. You employ fools and nitwits to do your bidding when you should undertake such things yourself; and quite clearly your assessment of character is equally below par, as is your attention to detail — both being qualities to which I pay the strictest attention when it comes to confidential reports... I do not wish to be harsh with you, Father O'Brien, but I seriously doubt if you will last the month."

Wakers Wakefield, the great Englishman, was everywhere that day: the Harlequin jigged and jogged and swerved his way to the line on two occasions, which set Maldwyn very dull and had the Bishop ecstatic, and he suddenly leaped to his feet with a roar like a bull as Wakefield came free and went over the Welsh line for a try.

"Sit down, ye Papish sack o' guts!" shouted Maldwyn, "the game's not over yet," and he elbowed my ribs. "Do you know what he said when I put him in the wrong hotel? He said there's never been a sane Welshman since Twm Shon Catti!"

The crowd had gone quiet, into deep mourning, "as always happens in Cardiff Arms Park when the opposition is flourishing," said the Bishop.

"Tell him to go to hell via Swansea," shouted Maldwyn, and got up and left us.

"Thank God he's gone," said the Bishop. "I have to say that you find your friends in some very strange places, O'Brien. And I shall need an explanation of this outrage, chapter and verse."

"Yes, my lord," said I.

The game had gone momentarily flat, when he added, "First impressions are important, as you know. And I am bound to say that friction already exists between us. And elemental disagreements are likely to transmit themselves to your parish, you understand?"

"Yes, my lord."

"It would be the greatest pity if we had to part company, O'Brien, for apart from your complete inability to assess characters, you appear to be a nice little man."

I thought of calling on God again at this stage, then remembered that he'd gone to China.

Meanwhile, the game, very dull by now, ebbed and flowed, and it looked as if Wakefield's single try would win the match. But fifteen minutes from the end England wilted under the attacks and George Andrews of Newport, making his debut, tapped a ball forward, chased it, snatched it up and went over the English line to level the score.

But thereafter England's fortunes changed and they were in constant possession: Wakers Wakefield was at it again. With the ball under his arm he went for the Welsh line with the pack in full cry. Hunting horns were being blown behind us, Union Jacks being waved, and the Bishop, frantic with expectation, was upon his feet, urging on his team. Wakefield, staggering on, was leaving a trail of dead and dying behind him; handing off Delehay, he was brought down by Harding, but in falling threw the longest ball I've ever seen to Voyce. And in the second before Voyce got his hands to it, a long, lanky figure in rugby kit dashed out from the touchline crowd: out of the mass came Maldwyn Thomas Rugby, intercepted the pass, tucked the ball under his arm and went like the clappers for the England line: against the run of the play he took that ball and went down the line like a bloody rocket.

Dead silence.

And then a howl of anguish arose from the England supporters, especially from my Bishop: cheers and catcalls from the Welsh now as Maldwyn went in a staggering, swaying run for touch with clods of turf sailing up from his size twelve boots, while the English Fifteen stood petrified and the Welshmen in red had collapsed, holding their stomachs, and my Bishop, poor soul, was in tears.

"My God, O'Brien," said he, "you've something to answer for," and he went down the aisle in search of Maldwyn Thomas Rugby.

They said they were going to build a chapel on the spot where Maldwyn went over, but they never did because the Selection Committee were against it: the Chairman, in his day, having been bottled twice by Maldwyn in the tap-room of the *Erin go*

Bragh for making the wrong selections.

It was snowing hard when I went over to Jim Driscoll's public for a tot or two to raise my flagging spirits. And who should be standing outside harnessed to the local knife-grinding and paraffin cart but Evan Pugh's billy goat. Mind, I'd already had a pint or two at the *Farmers Arms*, so I took off my hat and swept it low in the gutter at the animal's feet, saying:

"Good evening, ye foine creature. They tell me you're the Devil's parody, and by the look of you, this could well be. Is it you been doin' all these terrible things to me?"

And he looked at me, did Billy Goat, as if I'd just come out of Kibby's asylum, which wasn't far wrong, for I was at my lowest ebb, but I persisted:

"For one thing's certain — you're of the cloven hoof variety, so is it you been interfering in me future?"

Now the goat didn't reply, but I tell you this; there was a glint in that creature's eye that was mesmeric; with his horns sticking up and his straggling beard; with his two-inch teeth grinding he looked like something out of the infernal regions, and I heard strange noises in his throat. In that moment he was the essence of Beelzebub's diabolism; faintly I could hear the shriek of disembodied souls. I said to him:

"I'm tell you this, my son — if you're away over the Bobtail with paraffin for the Presbytery, confine it to that — just keep out of me private life. And if I discover you're at the bottom of my misfortune, I'll boot you from here to Cardiff General."

Just then Evan Pugh came out of the *Duke of Edinburgh* with a few pints aboard, too, and he staggered and doffed his cap to me. "Good evening," said he, slurred. "We're away, Billy and me, to drop a can of oil into the Presbytery, holy Father. Is there anything else I can do for you while I'm there?"

Friend or enemy?

I pushed past him into the *Duke of Edinburgh* to kill a few more pints.

"Dear God," said Jim Driscoll, holding me up. "I've never seen a holy man in such a state of disrepair — shall I see you back to the Presbytery?"

"Old Nick's after me, my friend," said I. "Pour me another pint, and lace it up with a whisky chaser."

It was past midnight when I got to my bed that night, and I awoke near dawn to a call of Nature, and opened the front door of the Presbytery hall. It was a night of besoms and blackness, I remember, with the stars so faint I thought they'd fall out of the sky; with Orion the Warrior rattling his sabres and Venus making the sign of the Cross. The wind moved, I remember, and the scarecrowed trees of winter began telling each other about the last beautiful summer. It was still snowing hard, I recall, but I saw something on the Presbytery drive.

I could see footprints in the snow that led down to the road; the shape of them took my eye, and I pulled my dressing-gown closer about me and went out into the night.

Bending, I peered down.

They were the imprints, not of a human shoe, but of a cloven hoof. Still faint, perhaps, but they were there. And then I remembered that Evan Pugh and Billy Goat had come round with the oil that night, so I nodded, relieved, and went indoors. Returning to my room, I lit the bedside lamp and was trying to drop into sleep by reading the *Parish Times,* when I heard a faint scratching at the door.

I put down the magazine, and watched, and the door moved, as if in a silent wind, and came ajar.

And there entered into the room in the flickering light of the bedside lamp the largest black cat I have ever seen: lanterns of amber it had for eyes and a tail a yard long; its mouth was drawn back so its teeth were bared; its fur was standing rigidly along the length of its spine. And even as I stared at the thing it slowly approached the bed in the slow, threatening crawl of a feline hunter. I shrieked and shrieked again, but no sound came forth, and I awoke in a ferment of sweat and terror, screaming my head off as a giant paw came over the edge of the bed. And awoke, with the face of a witch against mine and in the clutch of skinny arms.

"Father O'Brien!" cried Martha. "Oh, holy man, what ails ye?"

"Oh, my God!" I cried, sitting up.

"Is it a nightmare you're having, for heaven's sake. You've been wailing to wake the dead — sure, I heard ye right down in the kitchen."

And at that moment the bedside lamp flickered once more, and died.

"Ach, damn," ejaculated Martha. "I'll skin that Evan Pugh and his Billy — they were due last night with paraffin for the lamps, but they never came. The fella likes his ale, you know — like some I could mention."

Getting out of bed I followed her in the dark downstairs.

"The goat cart didn't come with the oil?" I asked.

"He hasn't been here for a week. Sure, I'll be happy in me heart, Father, when the lads come and fix the new electricity. O aye, and by the way. You had a visitor last night... *the new Bishop.* Ach, he's a darlin' man! He's bringing in a sweet Irish girl called Bridget O'Callaghan to help me with the chores!"

"Is he, now?" says I.

The telephone bell rang — at that time of the morning — and I lifted the receiver.

"I'm back," said God. "This is only to inform you, O'Brien, that your new Bishop arrives a week on Monday — and you'll be delighted to know that I've prevailed upon the Pope — the new one will be Irish after all. And the old one's had the sack."

"Ach, dear God," I whispered.

"Oh yes — and may I say, O'Brien, that you've done passably well. Your character assessment is better than I thought — you guessed who the other one was, they tell me."

"Aye, but it was easy," I replied. "The mark of the Fiend was written all over him — His Satanic Majesty can appear in many guises, as you know — even as an animal of cloven hoof or paw. He didn't know the first thing about rugby, I got that in one."

"And all he got out of you was two tickets for the International and a plate of faggots and peas!"

We laughed together.

"Who are ye talking to, holy man?" asked Martha, suddenly behind me.

"God," says I, and she fainted right off.

"Oh, and by the way, O'Brien," added God. "You probably don't know that we've got a thriving Fifteen up here. As you can guess, we actually invented the game. And we're playing old Beelzebub's lot at home a week next Monday... the Angel Gabriel is hooker and Peter's our stand-off. Incidentally, while we're on the subject, don't trust that Maldwyn Thomas too much, will you — indeed, I'd suggest you have a look at his boots next time you're close. For a man who'll intercept a pass at an International is likely to get up to anything."

• • •

Eastern Promise

'... he'd met this girl on the coast of Indo-China, smuggled her aboard his cargo ship somehow and brought her back to Cardiff, and every time she walked down Bute Street she stopped the traffic.'

• 4 •

Eastern Promise

In this world, especially if you're a parish Priest, it pays to think the best of people, but Patrick Magee was around pensionable age and the female he was consorting with was under nineteen. And, since there's no fool like an old fool, I decided to take a hand in Patrick's private affairs.

"Me old friend Patrick," said I in the bar of the *Royal Oak*, "Are you entirely off your nut?" and he removed his bowler and, without spilling his Guinness, bowed low to me.

"Father O'Brien," said he, "I can do nothin' about it, for the woman's a walking dream."

"Ach, you should be ashamed of yourself! The child's scarce out of the cradle, and you're too old a cockerel to be luxuriating in pastures of desire. You know where you'll finish up, don't you?"

And Pat drew himself up to his full five feet two. "Aye, holy man, but it'll be a wonderful death, so it will."

"And after that you'll go to Hell."

"Don't talk twaddle, Father," replied he. "My sins beside your powers of redemption is like hitching a po to the stern of the *Titanic*. Besides ..." and he patted himself to see if he was still there, for he was a frail old lad these days, "the sweet creature's after me marryin' her; she's pestering me morning, noon and night — she'll be after me again the moment I get in."

I stared at him. "Dear God, don't tell me you're living with her!"

"I am, and tomorrow morning I'm away to Mass, for nobody ever went to Hell on his knees."

"You should be ashamed, Pat Magee! Right under me nose and in me own parish! Heaven help us if the Bishop hears of it, so I'll be round tonight to inspect this she-devil who's led ye so far astray." I wagged a finger in his face. "And atonement don't come in half pints, remember."

"I know," said Patrick, "You try being a teetotaller in Wales."

Mind you, I had a lot of sympathy for old Pat; all his seagoing life a lonely batchelor, he'd met this girl on the coast of Indo-China, smuggled her aboard his cargo ship somehow and brought her back to Cardiff, and every time she walked down Bute Street she stopped the traffic. Only five feet high, she was just the right size for little Patrick, and people said she was a dream in miniature, with a split cheongsam skirt on her, a firm haunch, and eyes slanted so high that you thought they were never coming down: all this, according to Peg-Leg Jones, and he was over eighty. "The mice looking at her legs must be as big as quart glasses," said Ham Bone, the foreman docker, "And things ain't been the same since this foreign piece came to dockland ..."

But more, apparently, the women were getting it up their aprons, since everything on two legs in Irishtown had taken to midnight walks along Pendoylan, where Pat Magee lived with this darling of his heart. So, clearly, something had to be done. With my iron-tipped boots clattering on the pavement, I took myself down to Number Nine and hammered on the door with my brass-bound cane, and every curtain in the street went back, for it's not that the Irish are nosey beggars, it's just that they like to know what's going on.

Of one fact I was certain. If this wee Indo-Chinese lover didn't fit into the community of Irishtown, she was going back quick to the place she came from.

The door opened and Patrick's common law wife smiled at me in the redness of the dying sun, and such was her beauty that I thought it was the end of the earth.

"Good evening, holy man," she said, and knelt at my feet.

Ten seconds later she had ensnared me with her charm: a minute after that, as I sat in her spotless kitchen, she had decamped with my soul.

"Patrick is not at home, Father," said she in lovely English. "Shall we drink tea?"

"If ... if ye please, child, if you please ..."

Now she leaned towards me and the perfume of her swept my nostrils.

"Chinese tea ... Eastern Promise, it is called. Or English tea?"

"Make it Mazawattee," I replied, and prayed for the soul of Pat Magee, for at my present rate of delinquency the fella hadn't a chance.

"My name," she said, "is Ah Poo Chu ..."

"Dear me," said I, "that's a really beautiful name .."

"But my story, holy man, is a sad one. It begins when I was a child. Everybody in our little village was a tea-planter – oh, such a dear little village off the coast of Indo-China near Weri — you know this place?"

"No, Ah Poo."

My God, I thought, where the hell was Patrick.

She continued in a soft, husky voice, "After every harvest we would fill the bags and transport them on the village junk from the village to Port Weri, where the factory was located, you understand?"

Her slanted eyes met mine over the rim of her cup.

I nodded, and she went on, "But many bandits were located at places along the river, and these would stop the junk we were towing and make sport with us ..." And she bowed her head. "... and make us pay *Squeeze* to them before they would let us through."

"God in Heaven, what a world!"

"Often it would happen that the junk carrying the tea would be stopped six or seven times by different bandits, so that, by the time we reached Weri and the factory merchants, we had no tea to sell."

Tears came into her eyes.

"Don't upset yourself, ye dear thing," I whispered, and the very touch of her was like a brand on me fingers.

"Well ..." Ah Poo hesitated, staring at me. "Perhaps if I tell all these things, you will hate me, and ..."

"Tell me, child."

"Well ... our villagers began to starve. The bandits were squeezing us to death. So my parents formed a plan. They kept this plan secret from me and my twin brother Ling — we were then about seventeen. Ling was strong and brave and I gloried in his courage, and he forced my parents to tell us their intention, and it was this. We would sail at harvest time in the normal way, but this time we would not try to resist the bandits, we would not even try to dodge them by sailing at night. No ..." and with this Ah Poo stood up and the pride lay strong in her. " 'We will invite them aboard as friends,' said my father. 'We will tell them that, so poor are we, we have only enough for one guest — to eat and drink with us,' and this we did."

A silence came between us now and you could have cut junks out of that silence, such was its quiet. Ah Poo said, "What happened then is almost too horrible to relate. But understand this, holy man, I had no hand in it.

"At the first port of call we invited aboard our junk as a guest an old and terrible bandit whose name was Unc Chung. 'Come in, old gentleman,' said my father. 'Eat and drink with us, and look upon my lovely son and daughter. Is not my daughter fairer than a lotus? And need you return to your camp tonight? See now, how beautiful she is ...' "

I bowed my head, and Ah Poo said, "And while Unc Chung, that fat old bandit was leering at me, my mother brewed him this tea, which as I told you is called *Eastern Promise*, but in that cup she also mixed herbs and the crushed seeds of the oleander, a poison which leaves no trace." Ah Poo clasped her hands. "He died peacefully. Ling, my brother, helped my father to hide his body in the stern among the cargo bags, and then we set sail for the next bandit port of call, at which, again, we would have to pay

Squeeze."

"He was poisoned?"

"Was he not a bandit?" asked Ah Poo. "Had he not often killed for money, or even sport? But, nevertheless, he was a human being, and I wept for him and pleaded with my parents not to repeat this terrible crime, but they did. On and on we went down to Port Weri, and at every bandit camp we stopped, invited the chief aboard, and poisoned him. In the end we had more bandits than tea, and everybody laughed a lot about this — we only had three inches of freeboard ..!"

"And all those dead bodies?"

"Nine of them. Ling put stones around their necks and we buried them in the deep water of the sea a mile off Port Weri."

"Good God!"

Ah Poo resumed her seat and caught my hands.

"In your safe, peaceful Cardiff this sounds horrible, but life is cheap in Indo-China, as we were about to discover."

"You were caught?"

"Yes. The bandits tracked us down on our return home. First they killed my parents. After torturing my darling Ling, they hanged him before my eyes ..."

"And you?"

She covered her face. "They kept me as a hostage, and for their sport. But I escaped from them. For a week I wandered in the jungle, but then reached Weri. The *Osaka Maru* was in port there, a great ship for carrying tea, and from it my Patrick came ashore, and met me. The rest of the tale you know."

I had no words for her, but sat in silence. Ah Poo said:

"I am not a loose woman. My father would die of shame if he knew of me living here with Patrick. Also, I know of your rules, for I am missionary educated. But I beg you, holy man, do not send me back to my own people, just to die ..."

I drew Ah Poo to her feet. "Think no more about it," said I, "for I'll be having a word to the Bishop," and I was drying her tears when in comes Patrick himself with six pints aboard, and he didn't know if he was in Pendoylan or China.

"Pat Magee," I said in my nasty hard voice, "You're a disgustin' creature, so ye are, for thieving the virtue of this sweet, sad woman. You brought her here, so now you'll be marryin' her. You've made ye bed, Magee, so now you can lie on it."

"That's what's been worrying me," said Patrick.

So I married Ah Poo and Patrick in the month of June, and three months later met him in the *Royal Oak* on Broadway. Sure, I knew he was on his last legs when he pushed away his bitter.

"What ails ye, son?" I asked him.

"Father O'Brien," he replied, "I've bitten off more than I can chew, for I'm the mint sauce to Ah Poo's spring lamb, and I'm not lastin' the pace."

"Dear me, Patrick, me heart bleeds for you."

"Mind, the food's a lot to do with it, too," he continued. "I'm on winkles and Chinese cabbage three times a week. And the tea!" He made a face. "She calls it *Eastern Promise*."

"If I were you, I'd stick to Mazawattee."

Aye, the dear man was dying on his feet for sure, and come Christmas I was giving poor Patrick last rites, and the lovely Ah Poo Magee moved out of Irishtown and I never saw the going of her, for she was broken-hearted, and this I could well believe.

But around Christmas I was down in Swansea and we bumped into each other again, and I don't know who was the more surprised of the pair of us.

"Why Mrs Ah Poo Magee!" I cried, "the saints be praised!" for I was delighted, and she looked like a bride of twenty- four hours and twice as frisky: the tall handsome Oriental gent she had on her arm might have been all teeth and spectacles, but he had the light of love in his face.

Equal to any occasion, Ah Poo bowed low to me, saying, "Oh, dear Father O'Brien, how wonderful to see you again! This is my brave brother Ling I told you about, he has just joined me in Wales."

"That's marvellous," said I.

"Being my next of kin I was able to claim him, you see?"

I saw all right, but I could have sworn she'd told me they'd hanged him for dead in Indo-China, and I answered:

"So now you can both stay in Britain on your passport, eh? You've done well, Ah Poo."

"Yes, haven't I!" and she took my arm and the three of us walked off with me the pig in the middle. "Now, let's go home for a lovely cup of tea to celebrate our meeting," and she sent me a heaven of a smile.

"*Eastern Promise*, I suppose? No thanks, girl, I'm on Mazawattee. I've got me own views on your particular tea, and so has Pat Magee."

Ah Poo's eyes nearly disappeared in her golden face.

"Try proving it, Mister."

I didn't pursue it. After all, it pays to think the best of people and Patrick's demise was by natural causes ... unofficially hastened by a surfeit of affection, which is the way most men would like to go, including celibates.

For you don't meet Ah Poos every day of the week.

• • •

The Last Bare-knuckle

'From the *Blorenge Punchbowl* down near Abergavenny to the sporting yard of *The Boot* in Aberdare, he'd fought them all — twenty rounds a time for two guineas of a gentry purse.'

• 5 •

The Last Bare-knuckle

In my official capacity as Newtown's soul-saver I got to know Old Joe Waller, the mountain fighter, pretty well.

"Father O'Brien," said he, "When me time comes to turn up me toes in this world, do ye promise to give me the last rites?"

"Ach Joe," said I, "I'd fight the Pope himself for the privilege — when are you going?"

"When they put another penny on Skull Attack in the *Golden Cross*," said he.

Now the *Golden Cross* at the top of Bute Street in Cardiff's dockland was Old Joe's watering hole, and every night, wet or fine, you could see him knocking a bob in his Old Age pension: in his capacity as the official chucker-out he'd sit hunched in his corner by The Castle mosaic, glowering around the long bar from under his shaggy, jutting brows. Old Joe had fought them all — "four hundred fights," he used to say, "not including the ones I had with my Annie."

From the *Blorenge Punchbowl* down near Abergavenny to the sporting yard of *The Boot* in Aberdare, he'd fought them all — twenty rounds a time for two guineas of a gentry purse. He was still six feet up in socks, had a face for chopping firewood and a pair of cauliflower ears that brought tears to the eyes of Jim Driscoll. But it was peace at any price in the *Golden Cross* when Old Joe was there, even when young Carlo Fermente, the Italian heavyweight sensation who was flattening all and sundry in Wales about then, got up on the counter and yelled:

"I can lick any man in the world," which put the customers very dull and raised Joe's eyes above his pint of old and mild.

"Hey, landlord," yelled somebody. "Will ye order that fella down or we'll be seeing to him."

"Ach, leave him alone," said Joe, "He's only a lad."

Next moment, according to reports, a little Salvation Army lass comes in with her 'War Cry' and Carlo bends down, smacks her a kiss that knocks her hat off and brought every man in the place to his feet.

"Are ye all right, ye sweet thing?" asked Old Joe, putting her hat back on.

"Och, Joe, there's no damage," said she.

"He don't mean no offence, ye understand. He's just a big softy."

"Aye, sure."

And he looked into her face, did Old Joe, and saw in her smile the man he might have been.

Now Old Joe was a lonesome chap and he'd never been the same since his Annie passed on. I remember him cutting her thin bread and butter when I called on them in Canton just before she died, and his big, gnarled hands were trembling on the knife. He was a council roadsweeper, I recall, and his grand- daughter used to pass him with her nose in the air on her way to school.

"Aye, but he's got a sister somewhere, hasn't he?" asked Ocker Burns: it was a Friday night and we were killing a pint together in the *Golden Cross*.

"Yes," I replied, "over in Ely."

Just then Carlo Fermente arrived and jostled us; he'd made the *Cross* his training headquarters and looked like staying for good, and he cried, breathing Allsops all over us, "All right, all right — you have Driscoll, Welsh and Jimmy Wilde. But where are the big men? Do I have to fight pygmies?"

I said to Ocker, "Try to ignore it, have another pint."

"It's gone up again, ye know, holy Father," said a gnome at my elbow. "Threepence a pint, it's a blutty scandal."

"That's why I drink lemonade," said Ocker, "And Old Joe doesn't come in here since it went up in the Budget, you realise?"

"Old Joe Waller don't come no more because he's ill up in Ely," said the Irish gnome, and I reached for my hat.

"Why don't people tell me these things," I said, and I shoved young Carlo aside and went out into the night.

About a week later I was thinking about Old Joe; a strange combination, this one — gentleness and violence. Welsh to his toes, he spoke the language, and when he'd had a drop too much he'd stand to attention in the bar and give us *All Through the Night*.

He'd been given a trial in the front row at Cardiff Arms Park in his youth and wore a black armband when Wales was beaten, and every year, rain or fine, he made his pilgrimage to Builth to put a red rose on the stone of Llewellyn. Daffies he put on Annie's grave every Sunday and wore a leek in his hat on St. David's Day. And it happened that one morning I was standing on the steps of the Philharmonic Hall when I came across my old friend Ocker.

"Did ye hear about the rumpus in the *Golden Cross* the other night, Father?" he asked.

"A rumpus?"

People pressed about us in smells of hot cloth, lavender, mothballs: a few boots were squeaking, too, a sure sign they weren't paid for; the railway strike — tough in Cardiff about then.

Ocker continued, "Aye, all hell came loose just after you left, for Old Joe Waller comes in just when young Carlos was up on a chair singing *Land of My Fathers* in Italian, and Old Joe collared him, dragged him outside by the scruff and gave him an outing."

"Is that a fact?" said I. "What time would that be?"

"About nine o'clock," said Ocker. "They were patting the backs of Carlo's hands for ten minutes before he came round — I thought he was dead. Then Old Joe played hell with the landlord about that extra penny on a pint and went out saying he'd never come back."

"Did he now," said I.

We stood together in the sun ... in the silence of mutual friendship that has no call on words, and then Ocker, who was nobody's fool, said:

"Old Joe's passed on now, I hear, that right?"

I didn't reply at once because it was tricky. It was tricky, because it was about nine o'clock when Joe's sister let me into the house over in Ely, saying, "He's been asking for you, Father O'Brien." And Joe said from his bed:

"I'm away to see my Annie now, holy man," and died.

"What day did he die?" asked Ocker.

And I didn't reply to that, either: there are some facts left unproved and some things best unsaid.

Instead, I took Ocker over to the Badminton Club and bought him a half of Guinness. For it's a dreadful thing, as can well be believed, for a foreigner to sing *Land of my Fathers* in Italian.

• • •

Divine Intervention

‘ “It is astonishing to me,” said God, “how people mainly get down on their knees when they’re after something.” ’

• 6 •

Divine Intervention

Company Sergeant-majors come in different varieties, as is widely known by officers and men alike: some are such lovable creatures that those about them would die for them: others, mainly of unknown parentage, have been seen crawling out from under large stones. Our Sergeant-major came in the latter category, and was not known by his official name.

All ranks, from the regimental commander to the rawest recruit, called him The Black Mamba. This nickname, derived from one of India's most poisonous snakes when the regiment was stationed in Poona, had followed our Sergeant-major to the city of Cardiff, where I was unfortunate enough to meet him.

My story begins at the end of the First World War when our Second-in-Command, a Captain Wilson, put in for maternity leave and, dashing off to Cardiff station, tossed me the keys of the regimental safe, crying:

"Be a sport, Padre — pay the men for me tomorrow," and I shouted back:

"Willie, as a man of the Cloth, it's against the rules for me to undertake such a duty."

"Father O'Brien," said he at the door, "if we didn't bend the rules sometimes we'd break our necks. The Black Mamba knows all about it — in fact, he suggested it:" so, the moment he'd gone I found our Sergeant-major, saying:

"Captain Wilson's asked me to pay the men tomorrow. You

know about this, Sergeant-major?"

"Yes, Sir."

Smartly to attention was he, all five foot two of him; red-faced, bucolic, he was the terror of anything a rank below him and possessed a fawning obeisance even to junior officers. Children ran from him, recruits died of fright beneath the thunderous commands of his square-bashing voice, and rumour had it that he spent all his spare time up on Ely Racecourse gambling away money he couldn't afford, but I didn't know about this then as I tossed him the key of the Company safe, saying, "Then you'd better have this, Sergeant-major, I'm bound to lose it."

The Mamba's ginger moustache shone as if with an inner delight, and in an oily little voice, he replied:

"Thank you, Sir. Thank you for trusting me, Father O'Brien."

I should have had my head examined; it was the biggest mistake of my life.

At eight o'clock next morning I attended the pay parade where the men were lined up with glowing expectations of a night out on the town. But the Mamba, I noticed, wasn't himself. His fat little face stared back at me when I asked him for the key of the safe; a nerve in his temple was pulsating violently.

I repeated, "Come on, Sergeant-major. Give me the key of the safe and I'll get the money out ..."

He shifted nervous feet; the morning sun burned down in smells of boot polish, hot khaki and perspiration.

"Might ... might I have a word with you in private like, Father O'Brien ... ?"

"Of course. You look ill — are you all right?"

He took a breath like a man expiring. "You ... you shouldn't 'ave left the money in the safe overnight now, should ye ..? It's against the rules, Sir."

"I beg your pardon."

"And it's against regimental rules to give the key of the safe to anybody, Sir. The key's always kept by an officer, Sir ..." He sweated ominously, and so did I.

Behind him the men fidgeted and whispered: even they could see that the Black Mamba wasn't himself that morning. I said raucously:

"Are ... are you trying to tell me something, Sergeant-major?"

This stiffened him to attention, and he said officially, "The ... the money ain't no longer there, Sir, I regret to say."

"You regret to say? The money isn't there? What the blazes are you talking about, man? It was there yesterday. Six hundred and eighty-two pounds four and eightpence. We counted it together, remember?"

"That was yesterday morning, Sir. Now there's only four and eightpence."

I had the distinct impression that I was going to faint. Snatching the safe key from his nerveless hand, I swung back the door: two florins, a sixpence and two pennies sat there in lonely isolation on the top shelf.

"Good God," I ejaculated. "What's happened to it?"

The Black Mamba stared resolutely ahead, and said, "I 'ad a mental deterioration, Sir. I sometimes get 'em. Probably caused by malaria caught in the Gallipoli Campaign. War service, see? I'm more to be pitied than accused. Don't know what came over me, Sir. Took ten pounds of it and went up to Ely Racecourse for the afternoon ..."

"You did *what*?" Waves of increasing nausea were sweeping over me.

"Ely Racecourse, Sir. I likes a bit of a flutter, Sir, and when I lost the tenner I comes back for more, don't I, and borrows another fifty, an' that goes down the pan as well, so I comes back again and takes a hundred, and ..."

I took a deep breath. "Are you telling me, Mamba ... er Sergeant-major ... that you've stolen nearly seven hundred pounds of money to pay the men and lost it up on Ely Racecourse?"

He eyed me. "Now 'stolen' ain't a very nice word, is it, Padre, especially coming from you. I ain't a thief, ye know, I only borrowed the stuff."

I couldn't believe my ears. He added confidentially:

"I'll pay it back, Sir — I promise, Sir — every penny."

Visions were now assailing me. I was standing on the barrack square after my court-martial and undergoing official cashiering: somebody was snarling into my face and tearing off my tunic buttons while somebody else was stamping on my regimental cap. I said aloud:

"Meanwhile, will you tell me how we're going to pay the men?"

"Search me, Sir," replied the Mamba.

"What will you do when they arrest you, Sergeant-major?"

"Plead campaign sickness. Throw meself on the mercy of the Court, Sir."

"And what about me? Have you given a single thought about what will happen to me, you crass idiot?"

"I ain't got round to thinkin' about you, Sir," said the Mamba.

Clearly, this was a case for the Bishop. Somehow or other I would have to delay this pay parade until I could raise seven hundred pounds. New nightmares haunted me if I failed. Families would starve; there might even be a regimental mutiny. Cardiff itself might be infested by infuriated soldiers; blood could run in the gutters outside the Royal Oak Hotel in Broadway. And heaven knows what happened to holy Fathers who gave the keys of their safes to unadulterated bloody thieves like the Mamba, begging your pardon for the language, God. So I took a bus to Llandaff, safe in the knowledge that Bishops were full of grace for the poor and needy and earned thousands of pounds a year. But after I'd kissed the ring and told his Lordship the whole sorrowful tale, I took the 'bus back to Cardiff with the promise of a fiver from his post office book, the damned old skinflint. Therefore, back in barracks and on my knees in my room, I put the problem to God as succinctly as I could, for, as is widely known, He dislikes long administrative explanations.

"It is astonishing to me," said God, "how people mainly get down on their knees when they're after something."

"That's unfair," I replied. "In this profession I'm at it morning, noon and night, and you know it."

"Most professionals are," said God, dryly. "They range from bank clerks who've lifted the petty cash to city financiers out to make a killing on the Stock Exchange, but I didn't expect this from you." He sighed. "Actually I prefer mothers; they never pray for themselves, only for others. That's why I invented them — I can't be everywhere at once."

He was trying to change the subject, of course, so I asked, "Look, do you intend to help me, or not?"

There was a long silence; then, "You've been extremely careless, you know."

I bowed my head even lower. God said, "You know very well — or should do — that an officer never gives the keys of the regimental safe to a non-commissioned man, even a Sergeant-major. And he is a Sergeant-major, despite the stupid and cruel appellation you and your kind have accorded him. The Black Mamba, indeed! Apart from the personal insult, it's quite unfair to the snake. Further, and I'm afraid I have to say this, I prefer his forthright challenge to impending disaster a great deal more than your cringing obeisance. After all, nobody's going to shoot you for a mere seven hundred pounds, are they?"

"You don't know the Royal Artillery."

"And you could always offer to pay it back at so much a week when you're cashiered."

I looked up. "On my pay? The Bishop gets it all."

"Perfectly right and proper, and that's why he's a bishop, and I may say that I agree with every word of the lecture he gave you."

In desperation, I cried, "If I'm drummed out, a lot of the disgrace will fall upon you, you know. And the Church ..."

"Oh no, son, you're not hanging that one on me," said God. "That's blackmail. Listen to me, O'Brien." And He put on his nasty, hard voice. "If you think that Heaven is a sort of Department of Financial Appeal like the Income Tax Office, you've another think coming. You've made your bed and you're going to lie on it. Being a cleric doesn't give you licence to expect a bigger slice of divine intervention than that dispensed to normal people. Did you hear what I said, my man?"

He spoke on, but I scarcely heard Him, for I was down in St Mary Street holding up the local branch of Lloyds Bank Limited with the new Piat anti-tank gun, and running for cover stuffed with pound notes ... and then I heard God's voice:

"Yes, Father O'Brien, at the risk of repeating myself —*Divine Intervention*. For if every Priest down there with you applied by prayer for me to pay his mortgage or stupidly incurred debt, we'd be turned into a financial institution up here, as I've said before, and this I don't intend. Even the Pope's got problems in this direction, they tell me. You forged this situation through your own stupid error and you put that poor, unsuspecting Sergeant-major into an impossible moral position; frankly, my sympathy is all with him and there's little left over to spare for you. For to you, unlike him, I granted the powers of intelligence and human understanding, whilst all he got was a barrack square voice. To you I gave a strict moral code, but he was behind the door when this was handed out. So get up off your knees, O'Brien, and stop grovelling for favours, for he, unfortunately doesn't know how to pray. And do stop pestering your unfortunate Bishop, for I happen to know that his overdraft is as long as my arm, and to date he hasn't even mentioned it. Continue to beg when you should be fighting and it might even affect your ultimate immortality, remember: continue to snivel and your only hope might be to sneak in behind the children on Judgment Day. Now away, for I've had enough of you."

"Yes, Sir," I said, and rose, and a shaft of sunlight came through the room window and shone upon my face.

It's a queer old business, you know. I felt then as people always feel ... when they come out of church and stand talking in the sun. And a voice within me seemed to say, 'Go in peace, O'Brien,' so I went.

Well, to cut a long yarn short, I called the pay parade for six o'clock that evening, which would allow the lads to get out on to the town.

"But the money, Sir?" cried the Sergeant-major. "How can we pay the men without any money?"

"We've got the money, Sergeant-major," said I.

Now, I don't drink a lot, but I reckoned I deserved a pint after that, so I took a 'bus to the Docks and called into the *Duke of Edinburgh* which was run then by Jim Driscoll who had just come back from taking the featherweight title off little Joe Bowker at the National Sporting Club. And Jim, of course, was in the money for once.

"Thanks for the loan, Jim," said I, and gave him back the tenner he'd lent me that afternoon.

"Dear God," said he, "you've only just borrowed it — are ye sure you're all right for it, holy Father?"

"Aye, it served its purpose, Jim," and I blew the froth off my pint.

Jim smiled around the crowded tap-room. "Anyway a tenner's pin money in here tonight, you'll see. Most of the lads have just come back from the racecourse — and old Debbie Williams over there backed the winner at sixty-six to one," and he called over the room, "That right, Debbie? You won on the Welsh Grand National?"

The old boxer limped over to us. "That I did, Sir — what are ye having, Father? I picked the rank outsider ..." and he peered at me, his battered, ancient face an inch from mine. "Sure to God, didn't I see you at the same stand as me this very afternoon, putting a tenner on *Divine Intervention*, and me with ten bob in me hand?"

I replied, "Now, would ye be seeing a holy man on a race-course, Debbie. A man o' the Cloth? Come on, where's your sense?"

But he persisted, and his eyes, bright blue, stared into mine. "I saw ye, I tell ye — the spit and image of ye ... *Divine Intervention ...*"

"No Debbie," I answered. "You must be mixing me up with God."

The Phantom Match

'History has it that the fog dropped like a blanket on that match; that the players, in the end, were like phantom figures flitting to and fro; indeed, at one time it was so thick that the spectators couldn't even see the field.'

• 7 •

The Phantom Match

As parish Priest of Newtown, I've had to concern myself with fire-worshippers and other idolatrous pagans; exorcising and other queer occurrences. And over 50 years ago some strange things indeed were happening around Cardiff way, let me tell you.

But the strangest thing I ever came across — to date unexplained — was when Maldwyn Thomas Rugby, aged 80, dropped a goal up in Bristol in the Wales v England match.

A word of explanation:

Newtown at that time — it's gone now, of course — was like an Irish oasis in a Welsh community; but we, like the Welsh, were rugby mad. Anything could happen, mind, when Jim Driscoll fought Freddy Welsh of Pontypridd,but the balloon went up when the Welsh Fifteen tackled England.

Indeed, there was a bone of contention afoot when I called into the *Duke of Edinburgh*, the Driscoll pub, on the eve of the January 1908 International, and Maldwyn Thomas, the only Welshman in the place, was taking some stick off the Irish locals — he blew the froth off his pint as I entered.

"Ach, good evening, Father O'Brien," says he, doing me accent, which he'd got off pat, and added:

"Will ye tell these Irish numbskulls who's going to win the match on Saturday."

"England," I said, to start an argument. "The Welsh haven't a chance."

"Will ye have a bob on that, holy Father?"

Jim Driscoll poured my complimentary Guinness, for it's wrong for a man of the Cloth to pay for strong drink, and he said, "I'll trouble you, Maldwyn Thomas, to treat the Priest with more respect. Do you really think he'd lift a shilling out of ye pocket?"

"You could have fooled me," said Maldwyn, glum.

A word about this fella while on the subject:

He was as sane as the next one, save for the manner of his dress. Awaiting the call from the Welsh Selectors — this is what he said — seven days a week he wore full rugby kit; the red jersey, red socks and white shorts of Wales.

Once he was a wheel-tapper and the knocking got into his head, folks said. Now he reckoned he was the only sane one in the pub, which is some claim, when you're drinking with Irish.

Now he put his rugby boots on a table and folded his arms and looked around him.

"The letter's arrived," he announced.

"What letter?"

"From the Welsh Selectors — didn't I say it would? I'm playing for Wales up at Bristol next Saturday."

"What position?" asked somebody.

"Fly half."

"Don't be daft, Maldwyn," said I. "Percy Bush is playing fly half. I've just seen the team."

"Not now he isn't," came the reply.

"Can we see the letter, Maldwyn?" asked the landlord.

"Aye, son, I'll show it ye after the match. But right now I'm wanting a flutter on the result. Who's on?"

It was kinder to humour him. "Right, old gentleman," said I. "Drinks all round if Wales pulls it off — and I'll do the paying."

Maldwyn took a breath, got up, and stretched — he was a well-preserved man for 80, mind you. "Well," said he, "If I'm playing on Saturday I'd best take a trot up Leckwith Hill to loosen up. I always do six miles before breakfast, usually."

After he'd gone, a wag said, "If that fella's sane, then I'm half-way to Kibby's Asylum, so I am. Drinks all round is it? You can't lose, holy Father!"

"Yes, he can," said Maldwyn, putting his head around the door. "I already know the result."

Next Saturday afternoon, a bit before the kick-off in Bristol, I was crossing the Bobtail to the Presbytery for my dinner when little Minnie Cooney stopped me: she was 60, four foot six inches, and the heart of a saint beat under her rags, and it saddened my heart that she was a Methodist.

"Your Worship," said Minnie, bowing, "I was just coming over to St. Paul's to get ye. I knocked on Maldwyn Thomas's door to take him a bit o' dinner, and I found him real bad."

"Ill, you mean?"

"Well, he seems all right, but he's raving." She patted herself to see if she was still there. "There's no warmth in them rugby clothes he wears, you know — running around the Bobtail, kicking a ball about at his age — I reckon he's got a pneumatic chill."

"After my meal, I'll pop in to see him," I said.

When I entered Maldwyn's little house in 16 Ellen Street, he blew a whistle. "You're just in time, Father," he cried. "We've just kicked off," and he hitched up his white trews and lay back on the pillows. "It's a capacity crowd, you know — 25,000."

"That's foine, for this weather," I answered.

"You can say that again, mun — look, you can hardly see the posts."

He had the expression of a man who'd said nothing unusual.

Miss Cooney, his landlady, came up to me: she wrung her withered hands. "He's got his best set on for the International, you see?" and she patted his boot. "I was washing and ironing all last night. You've got to humour 'em, haven't you, your Worship? Will you take a cup of tea?"

"Aye, I will, thanks," said I. "It'll keep the Devil out," for queer things were happening on the bed.

Leaping about, Maldwyn cried, "Rhys Gabe has got it — he's running for the line!"

"Well done, Rhys," I said.

"But that bloody Slocock 'as pulled him down — the ball's gone loose. Get after it, Watts, you idiot! Get your skates on!"

Miss Cooney gave me the tea. "The language ain't too choice at times, your Honour, but he don't really mean it, you know, poor soul."

"I've heard worse," I replied, "Compose yourself, woman."

Maldwyn bellowed, "Winfield to O'Neill, O'Neill to Billy Trew, Billy Trew to Gibbs — let 'im go, you sod — look, he's got hold of his shirt!"

"*Jawch!*" whispered Miss Cooney. "He can come a lot worse, Father."

And Maldwyn yelled, "We've scored. A try! A try! The Welsh are over!" Screwing up his hands, he waved them about, with Miss Cooney patting and soothing him.

"Don't get excited, mun, try not to get excited ..." But he flung her off.

"Excited, ye silly bitch! Wales has a try, don't ye understand?"

I said, "Who's taking the conversion, Maldwyn?"

"Winfield, like I said. Oh, look! It's over!"

The match went on and the language got brisker. Miss Cooney said, a woman broken:

"Really speaking ye shouldn't be 'ere, holy Father, he turns up the really ripe stuff when he gets to the dressing room."

"Miss Cooney," I said, "Mr. Maldwyn Thomas is enjoying himself, and that is all that matters. Look, you get out and leave me to it."

"Hey, ref! Did you see that?" shouted Maldwyn. "It's a scrum. Hold 'em down, lads, oh, you dirty bugger!" Feet, Wales, feet, feet, *feet!*" And he kicked his boots about.

In all truth, and I must be honest, I was thoroughly enjoying the "match", and the adjectives were lending colour to the "spectacle". Rhys Gabe got another try. Percy Bush — oh what a man was that Percy Bush — was once again the Welsh genius, and O'Neill showed his incomparable individualism.

"Just look at that," said Maldwyn, suddenly. "The bloody fog's coming down!" he peered from the bed in my direction.

"Is it bad?" I asked.

"Bad, mun? We can hardly see the posts. I told you that before."

History has it that the fog dropped like a blanket on that match; that the players, in the end, were like phantom figures flitting to and fro; indeed, at one time it was so thick that the spectators couldn't even see the field.

"Pass it, *pass* it!" called Maldwyn. "Leave it, leave it. I'll take it, lads! Get outside me, Percy — and come on, ye fool, come on!"

I sat up in my chair as Maldwyn bawled, his two arms up. "Did you see that, Cooney? I've scored! I've dropped a goal. *I've scored!*"

"Bless his old heart," said Miss Cooney, and she smoothed Maldwyn's forehead as he lay back on the pillows. "He's fair worn out. He said an International would take it out of 'im."

I got up. "Ah well, he had a good match, God bless him. I'll call back after tea to see how he is, Miss Cooney."

"Bless 'im, he's gone to sleep, so he has," and she stroked his face, a woman calmed. But, when after tea I returned to the house, Miss Cooney was white-faced and trembling. Opening the door, she led me within the curtained room, saying:

"Mr. Thomas weren't asleep, holy Father. Mr. Thomas were dead. And just look at his nice clean jersey all torn an' all that mud on his nice, clean boots ..."

When I heard Jim Driscoll and his friends returning from the match, I went over to the *Duke of Edinburgh*.

"You won, I hear," I said.

"Aye, Father, we won. But what a match!" he replied. "The fog! It was like a phantom match — indeed the papers are already calling it that up in Bristol." He laughed. "And there was a devil of a barney at the end, when Percy Bush dropped that goal. The English claimed there were sixteen Welshmen on the field."

"I know," I said.

He stared at me as if I'd just come out of Kibby's Asylum. "Ye know?"

"Aye, and I know something more. Twenty-eight points to 18 was the final score, and Percy Bush never dropped that goal."

"Now beware mun — who did, then?"

I returned his stare, and he said, "Ach, come off it! I tell ye, I saw Percy do it. And if it weren't Percy Bush, it must have been God!"

"More than likely. Drinks all round," I said. "And here's to Maldwyn Thomas."

• • •

The Mills of God

'On my knees in my room that night I put the situation to God, and knew at once that He was in one of His club armchair impatient moods...'

• 8 •

The Mills of God

As you know, me name's Father O'Brien and I hail from County Cork, but since I've lived most o' me life down in Cardiff's dockland, the folk down here reckon I'm Welsh, which is fair, come to think of it, for Welshmen are only Irishmen who've never learned how to swim.

Now, towards the end o' the Great War I was a Chaplain to the Forces with the rank of Captain, and it was in this capacity that I tried to save the soul of Gunner Jake O'Hara, who came from Connemara.

He was a foine figure o' a man, this one: the women down Bute took one look and swooned right off: six foot up, he had a head o' black curls and dark-shadowed eyes that would bring a sigh to Satan. But the moment he came from the Recruiting Centre in St. Mary Street I knew we were bound for trouble; and so did the doctors who made him medical category 'C' — with the strong suggestion that he was light in the upper storey.

Being a man of God I decided to give this poor wreck me undivided attention.

It was the May of 1918. The Germans had crossed the River Marne and were fifty miles from Paris, so we needed every able-bodied man we could get our hands on. But the moment I saw Gunner O'Hara drilling on the parade ground I knew we were one man down, for he was the only fella in step — turning right when he should have been turning left.

Then the lads, not knowing the truth, started to get at him, and poor Jake O'Hara spent his nights wandering around with a brush and a bucket of ceiling whitening and written instructions to whitewash *The Last Post*.

But things really came to a head when our Sergeant-major (privately called The Black Mamba, after one of India's snakes) was told to call a full-dress Ceremonial Parade before the Regiment left for active service in France.

The sun had got his brass suit on, I remember: vivid rays of light slanted down on Tiger Bay, and the barracks was full of gay, chattering people, and the dais grandstand full of frilly lace wives and daughters and parasols, and the air was scented with the smell of lavender. Ach, dear me, women do smell beautiful.

" 'Morning, Padre!"

"Good morning, Ma'am!"

"Don't the men look absolutely splendid, Padre!"

Yes, Missus, I thought; I'll write home and tell ye how they look in the mud of Flanders in a month from now.

And then I saw our C.O. coming. With his monocle firmly clenched in his eye, Colonel Pellington-Smythe, D.S.O., M.C., fairly glowed with bonhomie.

" 'Morning, Padre! First-rate turn-out, what? Give Jerry hell when they get over there, eh?"

Faintly, in imagination, I heard the chattering of the machine-guns and the thumping of the Whizz-bangs, so I merely saluted. And was aware, almost immediately, of a presence at my elbow. Turning, I found the Black Mamba uncoiling himself nearby. His face was red with anger and his ginger, military moustache bristled with an inner Satanic fury.

"May I 'ave a word with you in private, like, Padre ... ?" he hissed.

"Why, of course," said I, returning his salute. "Something wrong?"

The Sergeant-major took a deep breath, "It's that Gunner O'Hara, Padre — one of your lot."

"One of my lot? What on earth do you mean?"

"An Irishman, ain't he? The only one in the Regiment."

Hostility was in the Mamba's voice, but I straightened without umbrage and looked at the fine body of men on the barrack square, waiting for the band to strike up the ceremonial passing out parade; like peas in a pod were they; bulging khaki chests and putties, white belts and boots like black glass ... all except Gunner O'Hara, who as the right-hand man was closest to the Mayor and Corporation, and only yards from Colonel Pellington-Smythe, who was to take the salute. The Mamba, close to fainting, said vacuously, his upper lip trembling:

"Gunner O'Hara, Sir. Can't you see? He's got on a *black* belt and *white* boots."

"Mark, Mary and Joseph!" I ejaculated.

Tears welled up in the Mamba's eyes. "He done it to do me, Sir. I told him to polish 'is boots with Cherry Blossom and pipeclay 'is belt ..."

"Ach, don't take on so, Sergeant-major," I said, and the Mamba whimpered:

"But I'll 'ave him. As God's me judge, I'll bloody 'ave him, beggin' ye pardon, Padre ..." and just then the stentorian voice of Colonel Pellington-Smythe bellowed from the dais, and the band, striking up, broke off on a minor key:

"Regimental Sergeant-major! Over here, if you please!"

"See ... ?" whimpered the Mamba, "he's done me. But I'll 'ave him. I'll 'ave that Gunner O'Hara — and more — I'll 'ave every Irishman in boots between 'ere and Sophia Gardens!"

"*Sergeant-major!*" The C.O. was now incensed, and the Mamba clattered his size elevens on the tarmac and bawled back:

"Comin', Sir. I'm comin' ..." And he whimpered as he went.

The next episode in Gunner O'Hara's life was horrific.

I was comin' out of the married quarters where the Orderly Corporal's wife had had a breach delivery, when her husband came running up.

"C.O.'s compliments, Padre. Would ye report to him in the Company Office?"

Once there in the holy of holies I was confronted by an irate Colonel Pellington-Smythe whose eyes, once a childlike blue, had been changed to a steely grey by long service, bad stations, good whisky and wicked women, and he said in frustrated anger:

"This mad Irishman of yours, Padre, he's in real trouble now!"

"Dear God, what's he done?"

The Colonel, being Sandhurst and therefore a total gentleman, was suddenly reticent; then, "Well, your ears will have to be offended, I suppose. Last night he called the Sergeant of the Guard a bastard."

"Ach, *no!*"

Now I didn't like this particular Sergeant, but there are limits to a Chaplain's mode of expression.

"And I want you to stand in when O'Hara appears on the charge, Padre," said the Colonel.

"Left, Right, Left, Right, Left! Prisoner and escort, halt — one-two!"

The Sergeant's voice nearly shattered my ear-drums: the office door crashed back and they entered like Barbarians through the gates of Rome.

"Prisoner and escort halt! Left turn! Look to ye front, O'Hara! *Look to ye front!*"

They clattered into silence: somewhere beyond the window a lark was singing. They had boots to shave in; khaki creases to cut their throats, red faces and short haircuts, and the Colonel adjusted his monocle and read from the charge sheet:

"Number 1869681. Gunner J. O'Hara ... Is that you?"

"Yes, Sir!" Smartly to attention was O'Hara. Handsome beggar.

"Charged under Section 40 of the Army Act in that he, on the 27th day of May, 1918, did call the Sergeant of the Guard a ..." The Colonel visibly faltered.

"A bastard, Sir!" finished the Mamba, nearby.

The Colonel looked up wearily. "Did you call him that?"

"Yes, Sir," announced O'Hara, and I wasn't sure, but I thought I detected the ghost of a smile upon his mouth.

"But why ... ?"

The reply was instant. "Because he is one, Sir!"

Behind the Colonel's back I smiled happily at the Sergeant of the Guard.

The Colonel raised a weary hand. "You are compounding your crime, O'Hara. Are you prepared to accept my punishment or do you want to go to court martial?"

"I'll accept your punishment, Sir."

Nothing mad about that, as far as I could see, and the Colonel's monocle dropped from his eye, and he said:

"Fourteen days C.B. March him out, Sergeant-major ..." and then he hesitated, which is always fatal.

Now the Colonel was essentially a kind man: his war record was excellent; he rode to hounds and played polo; was the son of a city financier; had an excellent family background. But now he delayed the dismissal with a wavering hand, saying:

"Is ... is there anything you'd like to say before you go, Gunner O'Hara?"

"Yes, Sir," said O'Hara. "You're a bastard, too."

The moon had killed the stars by the time I got into the *Duke of Edinburgh* that night. Now, I don't go a lot on the nose-varnish meself, but a tot o' two helps a fella to sleep. And Jim Driscoll, the famous boxer who ran the place, didn't reckon on disciples of the Deity paying for the hard stuff. And I'd just got me first

Johnny Walker down me when up comes a runner from the Company Office, and he swayed to attention before me, crying in a high soprano:

"Sergeant-major's compliments, Sir. Can ye come to the Sergeant's Mess straight away — it's urgent!"

"Sink that one, Father O'Brien," called Jim, polishing glasses, "and there'll be another waitin' for you when you're back." So I went.

It was a good job I did, for somebody had been going beserk in the Sergeants' Mess, with N.C.O.'s lying around like corpses and people pinching their cheeks and patting the backs of their hands to bring them round, and over in a corner the Provost Sergeant was getting the kiss of life.

"What happened?" I demanded, and the Mamba appeared from somewhere and bawled, coming to attention:

"Soldier went beserk, Sir. Came in 'ere on jankers for scrubbin', Sir. Somebody tripped over 'is bucket, Sir, and he ups and hits out at all and sundry, Sir, including his own Provost Sergeant," and there was the Provost Sergeant lolling on a chair and the Mamba lifted his regimental cap and the lump O'Hara had raised was as big as a duck's egg, and sparking. And Gunner O'Hara himself was leaning his backside against a wall and rubbing his knuckles, and humming a pretty Connemara tune.

I cried to the room, "But why bring me? This is a regimental matter!"

A voice interjected. O'Hara said, "I'd do it again, so I would, Padre. For they're beatin' me up in private and calling me a Dai Dafto, and they'll be havin' me in Kibby's Asylum before they've finished — and me with three certificates to say I'm sane and them with never a one among 'em!"

The Mamba bellowed into his face, "You're stark ravin' looney, O'Hara. But you're sane enough to strike Provost Sergeant, and him never done harm to a living soul! But I'm a different lad, my boy. I ..." and here he thumbed his chest and sprouted at the room. "I'm the middleweight champion of the Royal Army, my son. What's more, I'm not a Sergeant, I'm a Sergeant-major — a real, live Sergeant-major, my lad. Strike me!" And the fool closed his eyes and slanted his chin up and Gunner O'Hara took a regimental pace forward and hit the Mamba one that would have settled Jack Dempsey.

We thought he was dead; special prayers were said all over Cardiff; everybody in our Regiment hoping it was nothing trivial.

And Gunner O'Hara's feet didn't touch the deck.

"Can I speak to ye frankly in ye capacity as a man of God, holy Father?" asked Gunner O'Hara as I sat with him in the cell, awaiting his court martial.

"That ye can, me son," says I.

"I mean — can I talk as if I was in the Confessional, Sir?"

"Just open your heart, for I'm a Priest, my boy," says I, and he sat back in his chair. Regarding me with sober-serious eyes, he said:

"Ye realise, don't ye, that I've taken 'em for a ride?"

"Now now, calm yourself, me lad. Don't get excited ..."

"Ye see, I've taken them all in — the doctors, the medical boards, the military, me mates — even the Church. Ye must admit, holy man, it was a marvellous performance."

I stared at him.

"Ye understand, Father, I had to do it. For I've a degree in Biology from Dublin University; I've already got my B.Sc., and when I get out of here I'm after a Master of Science. Isn't that preferable to going to France and getting meself shot?"

I rose from my chair. "You mean ... ?"

"Do I have to spell it out to ye?"

"But ..." I began, "but what about your country? What about your mates who are dying out there? What about ... ?"

"Ach, damn me," ejaculated Gunner O'Hara. "Patriotism's the last refuge o' the coward, Father O'Brien! Ye didn't really think an intellectual chap like me could fall for that guff?"

I got to the door. "You'll forgive me if I leave ye to it. There's a wee smell in here that no man, or priest, can tolerate. Good night to you, O'Hara," and I left him to a conscience that never existed.

On my knees in my room that night I put the situation to God, and knew at once that He was in one of his club armchair impatient moods, for He said:

"Why is it, O'Brien, that every time your light goes on I know there'll be a storm in a tea-cup. You realise I've got a major war going on, I suppose?"

I replied, "Look, mine's the problem. I don't want to hear about yours."

"That's the trouble," said God, "nobody ever does. I've got half the human race intent upon blowing itself to pieces, I've got squabbling politicians by the thousand and war profiteers by the million. And everybody's on their knees, of course — even the Kaiser's praying. Now come on, for I haven't got all night — what is it?"

"I don't know what to do, Sir," I said.

There was a pause, then God said dryly, "Another prisoner of conscience? I've got plenty of those, O'Brien, I don't need another one."

Clasping my hands, I explained my predicament, and He huffed and heaved for a bit, then settled to listen, and said:

"You really do get yourself into the most astonishing situations! But don't try to tell me you don't know the answer to this one."

I said, looking up. "O'Hara told me the truth, but as a Priest I can't breathe a word to the authorities. Nevertheless, as a soldier and loyal to my country, I feel bound to tell my Commanding Officer."

"Nonsense!" said God. "Your loyalty is to me. O'Hara's off-loaded his conscience on to you, and you're trying to off-load it on to me. It won't wash, O'Brien, for it's weak, and you know it."

I said, "I was wondering, if I went to see the Bishop ... ?"

"You will not involve your unfortunate Bishop in this, O'Brien, you'll sort it out yourself. He's got a Convocation coming up and he doesn't want small dogs like you snapping at his heels — he collects enough stick from the Archbishop. Now go."

"I beg your pardon ..."

"Go, go, *go!*"

In desperation, I said, "But, don't you see; if I do nothing at all, O'Hara's going to get away with it!"

"Would you like a pint on it?"

It raised my face. "Any time you like. You mean you ..., you'll handle it ... ?"

"Oh dear," said God, "what a weak and colourless creature you are, O'Brien. You make a poor comparison with fighting Jake O'Hara."

So I leaned on Him, taking the coward's way out of my problem. But realised God had forgotten all about it when O'Hara got away with it at the court martial. He was sent back to Connemara under medical escort on grounds of mental instability.

A fortnight later, just before the Regiment sailed for France, I was in the *Duke of Edinburgh* getting into a tot or two of Johnny Walker, in commiseration of my weakness. And I was in the depth of a personal character assassination when a little fella comes into the spit and sawdust; not more than five feet high was he, with a bald head, a rhubarb smile, and a face like a Connemara leprechaun.

"Why, good evenin' to ye, holy Father!" cries he, and put his chin on the bar.

"Good evening," says I.

"Will ye glance out o' the window, holy man?" says he.

And I did so, and stared.

For there, coming down Bute Street to the barracks — and I had to rub my eyes to believe it — was Gunner Jake O'Hara in civilian clothes chained to a couple of burly military police.

The wee fella was standing beside me now, and he said, "He's a chap called Jake O'Hara, ye see. He tried to float his ticket by pretending to be daft. But Dublin University got hold of it ..."

He lifted his pint of Guinness.

"Aye, didn't you know about that?" asked Jim Driscoll, coming into the bar.

"Ach no! I've been away," I said, still staring.

"So they wrote to the Regiment," said Jim. "For ye can't be that daft if you've got a degree in biology, can ye?"

"And ye canna fool God, anyway," said the wee chap, and left us.

"Who's he?" I asked, after he'd gone.

"Search me," said Jim. "I've never seen him before," and he held out his hand. "But he knows you," he said, "and reckoned you owed him a pint. Fourpence, if ye don't mind — I'll give ye free drinks, but I'm not settling your bets."

After a bit I wandered out into the night.

"I'm obliged to ye, Sir," I said, looking at the stars.

There came no reply, and I understood why.

According to the *Church Times* terrible things were about to happen in the Balkans.

• • •

Fragrant Concubines

'Maldwyn Thomas Rugby was killing a quart when I entered Jim Driscoll's tap; dressed in rugby kit was he; white shorts, the red shirt of Wales with the feathers, and size ten boots — awaiting his call from the Welsh Selectors, and him aged eighty, the poor little dab.'

• 9 •

Fragrant Concubines

Many, many years after I first came, the poor folks around Cardiff's dockland were seeing more plates than dinners, and I was in trouble up to me eyes. Being the parish Priest, with the Deity blamed for everything from ankle-bracelet ladies to the price of Guinness, I was pig in the middle. But more. The Temperance Society had reported me for dropping off in the Confessional, Maldwyn Thomas Rugby was turning up for Mass in football kit, and Mr. Chan, the new Chinese owner of the Emporium, had been taken in adultery up in Dock Street. And so, with standards of morality dropping around my ears, I received an invitation from the new English Bishop to take afternoon tea over in Llandaff, which was practically a sentence of death.

I caught my housekeeper as she came into the Presbytery.

"Martha," I said, "the fella's on to me for sure. New English brooms sweep clean. Why the hell do they appoint English Bishops when they know God's an Irishman? I'm away to the knacker's yard."

"Retirement, is it?" cried Martha. "And will ye take it lying down? Where's the spunk in you, Father O'Brien? By the time I'm finished brushing and polishin' you, sure they won't know seventy from forty. Ach, forget the old spalpeen, come and have a cup of tea."

I tell you this, Martha O'Shea was a fine sweet woman: gaunt as a pile of haunches and shinbones now, perhaps, but time was she had a good plump leg on her: aye, thirty years back when she was Matron of the Theological College she turned every head in the street.

"What like is this new Bishop, then?" she asked now. "For if he's round about my time I surely must have known him, though his name doesn't ring a bell..."

"Oh, he's a big beefy chap," said I, "all bass booms and growls; a tower of a man, bald as a coot and with ears bigger than a blutty donkey's."

"Big ears, did you say..."

"And size fourteen boots. I'm away now, so I am. For if I'm taking tea with the monster this time tomorrow I'll have to settle this Chinese affair," and I took my leave of her.

"God go with ye, Sean O'Brien," said Martha, and flicked a speck of dust off me coat.

Ye know, the proposition that money never brought happiness is a yarn invented by the rich to keep the poor content, and Dockland could have done with a bit of spare cash about then. And I confess that I wasn't myself that afternoon going up Bute Street; the puddles were lifeless and sad at being out all night, and the sun that mean he was hired by the employers. Even Martha's blouse on the Bobtail washing-line had its hand in my trouser pocket as they flapped in the sea wind, and the women were scragged back and talking in whispers, always a sign that things are wrong in town. For the women of Irishtown are the centre of the earth in more ways than one, and things are dull when they cease to be vociferous. Aye, my mood was poor, and I mentioned this to myself in passing: 'Sure to God,' I said to meself, 'if I'd known what this world was going to be, given the option I'd never have come into it.' "

"That's a terrible, ungrateful thing to say," said God.

I paused outside the *Duke of Edinburgh*, which was Peerless Jim Driscoll's pub. "I didn't specifically refer the remark to you, Your Worship," said I at the sun.

"I should hope not," replied God. "Compared with some folks round here, you clerics have never had it so good."

"That's your opinion," said I. "Isn't the situation bad enough? Did you really have to send me an English Bishop?"

"Ah, so that's it! All Bishops have to be Irish now, eh? Next you'll be wanting the confirmation of Dublin."

"You could do worse. I've only talked to this English spalpeen once. He'd never heard of the '98 and he thought Father John Murphy had a parish in Swansea. Have you got Oliver Cromwell up there, or something?"

I got going, for the temper was on me.

"And where might you be off to?" asked God. "The minute things go wrong it's the demon drink, isn't it? Dear me, you have to kill a hundred Irishmen to get a pound of brains — the man'll smell your breath, so he will."

"That's blackmail," I shouted up.

"If I tip him off it'll be diplomacy," said God.

Maldwyn Thomas Rugby was killing a quart when I entered Jim Driscoll's tap: dressed in rugby kit was he; white shorts, the red shirt of Wales with the feather, and size ten boots — awaiting his call from the Welsh Selectors, and him aged eighty, the poor little dab.

"How are you, holy Father?" cried he in his falsetto valley Welsh.

"Fair to middlin'," and as Jim came up I said, "A pint of sarsaparilla and a three inch livener under the counter, for God's sake."

"Your mood's poor, Father?" asked Jim.

"Me mood's excellent, but there's informers all over the place," and I sank the Johnnie Walker under cover and put the sarsaparilla on the counter.

"Is there something on your mind?" asked Jim.

Ach, he was a fella and a half was this one; County Cork Irish and an eye for the poor and needy such as penniless parish priests, for he was the unofficial featherweight champion of the world.

"There is," I said. "It's a one-ton English Bishop about two feet between the eyes. The man's after retiring me prematurely and me fifty years in the same pulpit."

"But what have you done?"

"Ach, I dropped off during a Chamber of Trade confessional and he's been listening to the slanders about the Chans up in Dock Street."

"Sure, it's a bundle of lies about the Chinese Chans, Holy Father!" bawled Maldwyn Thomas Rugby, taking me off. "Don't ye know the Orientals are related to the Welsh and the nations are respectable. And I'm playing scrum-half for Wales up at Twickenham next Saturday."

And I shouted to Jim:

"God help me, I'll be having his life. Will you get him into a jumble sale suit before he comes to the altar next Sunday, for that fella's half me trouble."

"But he's right," said Jim. "Mr. Chan's a most respectable chap; he's a wife and three daughters and as timorous as a mouse. What's wrong with him?"

"Three daughters, is it? Three active concubines, ye mean. The scandal's flying and the Bishop's got hold of it — immorality in O'Brien's constituency, he calls it, and he's after me blood."

I sank the next whisky after a quick look around for John Wesley. "I'm taking tea with him tomorrow, which means I'm out on me neck."

"Jesus, Mary and Joseph," whispered Jim. "Tea with that monster. I'd rather go fifteen rounds with Jack Dempsey. Ye'd best have another, ye dear man."

"If ye insist on it," called Maldwyn Thomas Rugby, taking me off again. "May the blessing of God be upon ye for the sweet Irish fellas ye are."

"Try to ignore it," said Jim.

I judged Mr. Chan's age at sixty. As bald as an egg, for the curse of wealth crops them closer than shears, he rose in his long, black mandarin gown and bowed to me with regal dignity as I entered his drawing-room. In perfect English, he said:

"Welcome to my house, holy man."

Behind him, arrayed in the white Shantung silk that denotes purity, stood three of the most beautiful earthly creatures it's been me privilege to set eyes upon, the concubines.

Like peas in a pod were they, with black hair down to their waists, almond eyes, golden faces ... and inflated by Nature into exactly the right proportions. Hovering at the door was a blue-clad coolie amah, presumably a servant. Incense and perfume pervaded the air; the walls were decorated with jade paintings and gilded Chinese gods.

Shaking hands with himself, Mr. Chan said:

"May I present my family, Father O'Brien. Firstly, Tai Tai, who is my wife," and he indicated the coolie at the door. "Next, First concubine Pei Sha; Orla Gold Sister, and Suelen Water Lily, my three little stars."

And down they went in deep, respectful bows: their perfume, mixing with the sarsaparilla, was having a profound effect upon me.

"And now, presumably, you would like to speak privately?"

Alone with him now, I said in my nasty hard voice, "I suppose you know why I'm here, Mr. Chan? There's a gale of scandal flyin' around Irishtown since you came."

"How could it be otherwise, sir? Does not all calamity arrive by means of the mouth?"

"Aye, but spare me the Confucian ethics, man. In a civilised society you conform to certain civilised standards, or perhaps I'm mistaken."

He peered at me. "Civilised, did you say? China was civilised while you were beating your wives with clubs."

"Ach, to the devil wi' all that," said I. "When you're in Rome you do as Rome does, and that doesn't include supporting three active mistresses."

And Mr. Chan rose from his chair, and said coldly:

"What is a mistress in your country, sir, is a wife in mine. Under the law of To Kwong I am permitted as many wives as I wish, and all my marriages have been sanctified under the laws of Hong Kong."

"Ay ay, foine and dandy, son. But you're not in Hong Kong now; this is Irishtown. And while there's thousands of one-wife Chinese living in Wales, the Bishop's got hold of your custom marriage, so you're in trouble, and so am I."

"Besides," said he, ignoring this. "What right have you to invade the privacy of my life? It is insulting that I should be accused of cohabiting with young concubines who are little more than children. My *tsip* is called Tai Tai; she is my wife and the others are in service to her, to mend and cook and clean. 'A wife is like a pony bought, and I will ride and whip her as I will,' says Confucius. But he has been a long time dead, and I come from the new Hong Kong. Who are you to accuse me of sullying childhood? How dare you!"

Officially degraded and dismissed, I met the three Fragrant Concubines at the door, and they looked at me like Delilah looked at Samson before she blew the candle out.

"Platonic, holy man?" lisped Pei Sha, the eldest. "Of course, Mr. Chan and us girls, velly, velly platonic."

And I was out of that house like the Devil with St. Peter behind him.

"You made a right mess o' that one now, didn't you?" said God.

Tea with the Bishop next day was worse than I'd expected. Warming his behind at the fire, he was all gas and gaiters with an Oxford accent and I could tell he was determined upon my demise. No more falling to sleep in the Confessional, said he: Maldwyn Thomas Rugby would come properly dressed to Mass or he was off to the nearest nonconformist Calfaria via Twickenham, and he'd give me an extension of six months to see how the Chans turned out.

While cycling back to Irishtown I looked at the sky.

"A six month extension, and I can't say you helped a lot."

"Frankly, I'd have given you three," said God. "Your parish discipline is poor, you have an avid disregard for the wealthier classes, your administration is practically nil, and you drink too much. And after all......." and here he paused. "At the age of seventy plus you are bound to be failing."

"Have you stopped to think that you're getting on yourself?"

"I'm Omnipotent," said God, "and you are not; the theorem doesn't apply."

When cornered he always pulled rank on me. I said, "So you're not going to help me? Yet you've got an old reprobate over in Swansea and he's knocking ninety."

It began to rain and I got soaked; another of his tricks. And I thought he'd gone, when suddenly he said:

"You never could stand on your own feet, O'Brien. May I suggest you hand things over to Martha?"

"Martha?" I stared up. "What's she got to do with it?"

"You'd be surprised," said God.

Come spring, brightly coloured birds were flying over the old Taff and the lovely current bun was making love to the earth. The winter was over and I'd forgotten my impending retirement when a knock came on the Presbytery door, and who should be standing there but the lovely Fragrant Concubines, the Chans — Pei Sha, Orla Gold Sister and Suelen Water Lily — and all were just about as pregnant as concubines can be.

"Well, well, well!" says I. "Congratulations, all three!" and Pei Sha, the eldest, said in her lisping English:

"When our babies come out, you baptise them in your faith, holy man?"

"Why, of course, ye darlin' things!"

"And us, too?" asked Orla Gold Sister. "You baptise us as well?"

"Now, would I leave ye out? Bring your husbands, too; the more the merrier!"

"Mr. Chan is our husband. And he do not wish for English baptism."

I stared at them.

"Holy smoke," said I.

"Oh dear me," whispered Martha when I told her. "Now we're in trouble for the administration's collapsed again. But, I'm in this, too, you know — if you go, I go, too. But, I've got a sweet idea, though it does mean hitting a bit below the belt......"

"If the belt belongs to the Bishop, count me in," said I.

"Well," said Martha, all dreamy. "I've been wondering for months where I'd seen the Bishop before, and this morning I got it." She clicked her fingers. "You want to stay in the job, I want to stay as your housekeeper. So will you, from now on, do exactly as I tell you."

I sighed. "It's already been suggested. Proceed."

"Then sit down at that desk and write precisely what I dictate," and she dictated, and I wrote:

> 'Your Grace,
> I have received your instruction to retire from
> this office at the end of next month. But I have
> decided, with respect, to stay in post until
> the good Lord Himself dispenses with me
> permanently.

Incidently, had I known this was only a temporary position I'd not have taken it in the first place.

Father Sean O'Brien.'

"That won't work," I said to Martha. "He'll merely tear it up."

"Oh, no, he won't," she replied. "You see, before he was ordained and attending the Theological College, I was the junior housekeeper there. Mind you, I was a bit more presentable then. Indeed...." and here she smoothed down her bodice and fluffed up her hair... "I was looked upon as a very desirable little bit of fluff. So put this note in with your letter to the Bishop because I've recently remembered something about His Grace... *Big ears...*" and she waggled hers at me.

"Great big ears like errant wings, the darlin'," and I took the note from her and read aloud:

> 'To Bunnylugs, with love from his little
> Roly-Poly, remember? I'm getting the
> push here; can I come and be your
> housekeeper?'

On my way up Bute Street to post the letter a clap of thunder rolled across the sky, but I ignored it.

And then I heard a deep voice say:

"That, O'Brien, is absolutely outrageous!"

"Yes, I know," said I. "I wonder who put the she-devil up to it?"

I got no reply. Not that I expected one.

• • •

Adam's Sin

'Ale has more than one way out of a man, and another is through the eyes, so I didn't weep for Tilly O'Shea, my first and only love.'

• 10 •

Adam's Sin

The general public don't give a lot of thought to the man beneath the black cassock of the Priest. How can it be, folks think, that there exists in a Papal sack of guts a beating human heart and a body frought with the human desires that uplift or pester a normal working fella?

Now you think again, I tell 'em, a man's a man for all that.

The yarn I'm going to spin takes some believing, but I pledge it to be true on a baby's life, for it happened soon after I was ordained at the age of twenty-four, when I came to my first living in the parish of Tiger Bay, down in Cardiff's dockland.

Yes, I was as normal as the next chap: I'd collected a thick ear playing scrum-half at University, I liked a pint at the *Duke of Edinburgh*, and the sight of a pair of silk stockings blowing on a wash-line was inclined to send me feverish. Likewise, my heart always beat a bit faster when the District Nurse cycled by.

For such reasons, I plunged myself head first into parish work, since the Devil finds work for idle hands.

Now, I'm very fond of children. And I like nothing better than to go down Dock Street with a toddler on each hand and others coming up behind all stuck up with toffee apples, for the kids in my time didn't get a lot in Tiger Bay. Later, when they grow to adolescence, I watch them again, with joy: see them escorting each other in the magic lantern shows in Park Hall, snogging in the back rows; the lads with polished faces and their hair smarmed down with condensed milk, their eyes like organ stops; the lassies with their noses stuck up into the Nestles. I tell you, they're marvellous, and I was always down on my knees bumping the hassock, begging for something on their behalf.

"You know, Father O'Brien," said God. "Every time your light goes on I know I'm going to be touched — do you think I'm made of money?"

"I'm needin' thirty pounds for the Children's Outing to Barry next month," I replied.

"I sent you twenty a week last Monday."

"That was for the Mother's Union, Your Reverence."

"Heaven preserve us," said God. "I've got an earthquake in Peru, a Convocation in Canterbury, a famine in Africa and the Pope's got the auditors in again. What's more, I'm just off to China. Is there anything else while you're at it?"

"Yes. You promised me a housekeeper, Sir."

I was a bit nervous asking for this, because he had his nasty hard voice on again, which meant that he wasn't to be tampered with, but he was most accommodating, saying, "Oh yes, so I did. I'll send old Martha along when she's free. Unfortunately, she's with the Anglicans at the moment, but she's the one for you — keep you on the straight and narrow."

"I was hoping for somebody younger," said I.

"Oh, you were, eh? Listen. It's prime beef for the bishops and rag-bags for the curates, that's the administration rule. I've had some poor experiences with you young gadabouts, so it's old Martha, or nothing."

She'd seen better days, had Martha. Give her a broom and she'd have been up and around the chimneys. Still, when you're first ordained, you've got to take what you can get.

Now, there's two certain sins that trespass against the laws of St. Peter for a priest: one is gambling, the other is raising an eye at the female of the species. So, imagine my surprise when I called into the *Duke of Edinburgh* for a glass of ginger ale and Jim Driscoll, the landlord, told me I'd drawn a horse in the forthcoming Irish Sweepstake.

"You're ravin', man," said I. "I didn't buy a ticket."

"Maybe not," replied Jim, "but I did — in your name," and he waved the ticket in front of my Guinness. "What's more, you're straight into the money, holy Father, for the Dublin agent's just arrived and he's offering you a hundred pounds for your chances," and he nodded to a chap in the tap-room; a big burly fella wearing a yellow waistcoat and a face like a navvy's arm-pit. "Isn't that right, Swillikin' Jock? Ye'll hand the Priest a hundred nicker in exchange for his ticket?"

"Snap on the nail," said Swillikin' Jock, "like Resurrection Day," and he slapped a hundred pounds down on the counter.

"What's the name of the horse I've drawn?" I asked.

"*Adam's Sin*," said Jim Driscoll.

"That settles it," said I, finishing my Guinness. "Gambling's against the rules of the church, though I'm obliged to you. One mistake's already been made, I'm not contriving another," and I sank my glass and went out into the spring sunlight.

The second temptation came not a week later, which was reasonable since St. Peter's testings always arrive in bunches when a young priest is on probation, and this time he caught me napping.

But first let me clear a point with you.

Never could you call me God's gift to women.

I had flat feet, wore steel-rimmed spectacles, was as plump as a

Christmas goose and a penniless celibate. Nevertheless, as a lover of Mankind, I'd have sacrificed myself on the altar of womanhood seven days a week, just to keep 'em happy.

But the female standing on my Presbytery steps when I got home one night fair took me breath: she was a sudden and passionate affirmation of what life ought to be.

"Good evening, Father O'Brien," said she, and bobbed a curtsey.

Had the wealth of Sodom and Gomorrah been poured at my feet then, I'd not have lowered an eye. How to tell of her with only words to use?

"My name's Tilly O'Shea," she said. "They tell me you're after a housekeeper, so I've come to apply, so I have," and her voice was as husky as the lower cleff of a Handel contralto.

In with her quick before she changed her mind.

"Now, I don't know how ye managed that," I said to the altar when I got into the Presbytery, "but I'm very much obliged to Your Reverence for not sending me scraggy old Martha."

I didn't get a reply to that, nor expected one, for I knew He was away somewhere — either in Rome with the Pope, or Peru, or China.

For all her marvellous beauty, she was a frisky little piece, this Tilly O'Shea and after a week or so as my housekeeper I felt I'd known her all my life, for her steak and kidney was the best I'd ever tasted and her spotted dick fit for the Pope himself. And, I tell ye this — the girl smelled beautiful; as if she had washed her body in musk and pinned sprigs of lavender on her petticoats. Her hair was black and wreathed down over her shoulders, but best of all was her eyes.

It was her eyes.

Within their depths lay the serenity of a madonna, and were full of suffering. And there grew out of that suffering an affinity between us that surely was the will of God. Perhaps, I considered, since I was proving myself no great shakes as his worldly representative, the Man in the Big Pew was easing me out with my cards. For I spent my days wandering lost: in a daze when I should have been awake, awake when I should have been asleep, for the woman was playing Hamlet with my priestly biology. For the first time in my life, I was in love. And so, a few days before the Sweepstake race was to be run, I went down into the kitchen below stairs to bring matters to a head, and found the dear thing down on her knees and scrubbing.

"Miss O'Shea," I said to her, "I've something of importance to say concerning the pair of us. So will ye oblige me by serving dinner for the two of us upstairs, and I'll open us a bottle of wine..."

And she got to her feet, did Tilly, wiped her hands on her pinny and said in a voice like Anthony and Cleopatra, "Ach, ye dear sweet man, Sean O'Brien. Sure to God, I thought you'd never ask."

I was sitting there at table awaiting Tilly O'Shea when she came into the room, and the cut of her gown was like Clara Bow's nightdress; white for purity and with a splendid prow on her, and she walked like a Nubian princess.

"Miss O'Shea," I said, taking her hands, "I've fallen mad in love with ye, God forgive me, and I've drawn a horse in the Irish Sweep which is running next Monday. Is it too much to ask if you'll be me wife?"

"Mercy and Providence spare us!" she exclaimed. "You haven't!"

"Haven't what?" I asked.

"Drawn a horse? Ye haven't!"

"I have," said I. "And I'll tell ye something else. If the nag wins I'll deck you out in silk and finery and leave the clergy entirely and take you off to the Bahamas with me; now then!.."

And I filled up her glass, for I was seeing two of her, and but for that I'd have known she was crying.

"Ach, no, girl! What's wrong with ye?" I drew her to her feet and in my arms I held her, and the effect had a terrible drain on my constitution, for I had never had a woman in my arms before. Weeping buckets, the poor soul said:

"Oh, Sean O'Brien, I love you, too. From the moment I set eyes on you. But can't you see that money would be the ruin of us? Can't you see that it would be the end of the magic? I've suffered once before with having too much money and I'm having no truck with the filthy stuff again. Money would part us for sure. What's the name o' the nag?"

"*Adam's Sin*,"

This set her off again. "And you a priest? If the thing won we'd be cursed, so tear the ticket up just to please me, is it?"

This set me thinking. "Mind, I could sell the ticket for a hundred pounds — enough for the Children's Outing over the next couple of years..."

"Then do that," said Tilly, and kissed my cheek. "And while you're wondering about that I'll slip downstairs, so I will, and get into something comfortable."

While Tilly was downstairs decking herself up, a voice came through, saying, "I'm just back from Peru, Sean O'Brien. What's happening down there?"

"Nothin', Your Worship," said I, covering up the bottle.

"Is that a fact? I'm back, and not a moment too soon, ye varmint. Within the week you've cornered a woman, you're guzzling wine, and you've drawn a horse in the Irish Sweep. Another two hours and you'd be riding round Tiger Bay on the back of a pig."

"I'm innocent of all charges," I replied. "The ticket was bought for me, it's not Communion wine, and I'm above the charms of women."

"You could have fooled me," said God. "Also, you're drunk, O'Brien. I'll see you when I get back from China. Meanwhile, put a cork in that bottle and get rid of the woman."

"Sure, I'll do me level best, Your Worship, but I can't guarantee anything," I cried, and he hadn't been gone ten seconds when the door-bell rang and Swillikin' Jock, the big, brutal Sweep agent called.

"Have ye made up your mind about selling that ticket, holy Father?" he asked.

"Give me a hundred pounds and the damned thing's yours," I answered, and counted the money. "Sure to God, it's more trouble than it's worth."

Next morning I was in the bar of the *Duke of Edinburgh* after a hair of the dog that bit me, and Jim Driscoll asked:

"Have ye had breakfast? For it's criminal to drink on an empty stomach, Father," and I replied:

"I'm away for it now, my son: that sweet thing Tilly O'Shea will be cookin' it, without a doubt."

"I don't believe so," said Jim, "because I've just seen her and Swillikin' Jock carrying suitcases on their way to Cardiff station. Didn't you know those two were as thick as two thieves?"

"Holy God, I did not! What's happening?"

"Search me," said Jim. "The fella was rough and tough with her, and the wee thing was crying her heart out — I tell ye, I nearly interfered..." and here Jim paused and eyed me. "You... you didn't sell him the ticket, did you? For *Adam's Sin* has just come through at evens and ye stand to collect a fortune..."

I made no reply to this, for it's never wise to make two fools of yourself in under a minute.

Ale has more than one way out of a man, and another is through the eyes, so I didn't weep for Tilly O'Shea, my first and only love. But sometimes, even now, all these years later, I give a thought to those full red lips; for while young men have their visions and old men their phantasies, very old men are entitled to phantasies as well.

And after leaving Jim that morning I had a stroll down Bute Street with a toddler on each hand, and watched the lovers, and looked upon their sweetness with a new, unjaundiced eye.

"I'm sorry about the O'Shea woman," said God. "I was away, you know, and can't be everywhere at once."

"Ach, that's all right, it's all good experience, but I'm surprised you let the pair of them get away with it. According to Jim Driscoll they would be into a fortune."

"Oh no, they won't," said God, "*Adam's Sin* just broke a leg. Fifty thousand pounds? I want that money for the China Inland Mission." And he added, "But you'll do all right, O'Brien, for your reward's in Heaven," and I went back home and found old Martha waiting on the doorstep.

• • •

Caesar's Wife

'Unaccountably, I put my arms about her, and such was the sudden radiance of her face that I thought Jesus might have touched her; and she was soft and warm against me so that I remembered again our youth in Connemara.'

• 11 •

Caesar's Wife

Cardiff's Dockland around Tiger Bay was a melting-pot of a score of different nationalities after the Great War. In my capacity as its parish Priest I've married Japanese to Scots and Germans to Balinese; I've birthed them, baptised them, married them and buried them — lovely creatures one and all, but I tell you this: I never saw one to compare with Bridget Mary O'Callaghan, me old friend from Ballacroy on the coast of Connemara. I'd known her since she was a two foot baby, but the sight of her now in full womanhood nearly took me breath.

Now then. This was about the time I started the Charabanc Sundays — annual outings to Barry for deprived children of the docks, and with Bridget's arrival here there came hunting a fine looking specimen of a fella called Caesar Correlli. And Bridget took one look and fell on her ear. Caesar courted her, won her, and I married them in St. Paul's with a lump in my throat. And after the wedding reception I slipped into Jim Driscoll's pub for a quart of skull attack to drown me sorrows.

"Ye know, Father O'Brien," said Jim, "I smell a rat in this Caesar Correlli. His mither should have thrown out the baby and kept the stork."

"Aw, come off it, Boxer — that's a terrible slander on a fella."

"Is it?" Now this man didn't mince his words. "He was in here the other night telling the room, 'I'm taking on the lovely Bridget, lads, but she can send her baby elsewhere. All the boys going up my stairs are going to be Italian.' " And Jim peered at him. "I didn't know the sweet woman had been married before."

"She hasn't," I told my ale.

"The lad's illegitimate?"

"There's degrees of that, Jim, since she happened to love his father, who was killed — let's leave it at that, shall we?" and I went out into the spring sunlight.

Now, Bridget Mary had saved a couple of hundred pounds in her Post Office book, and with this Caesar, who was penniless, opened an ice-cream parlour down the docks, then another, then more. Then he formed a partnership with some randy old toffs in the Stock Exchange and invested his money in unseaworthy ships which sank at the cost of sailors' lives, so naturally made a fortune. He bought a mansion in Radyr, shooting rights down Rheola and a mile of fishing on the Wye. To and from Mount Stuart Square every day went Caesar Correlli in an open landau with two white horses; he waxed richer and fatter while poor Bridget became plainer and smaller, dying inside. Because her man was also investing in mistresses and paramours, totting up his profits by day and his harlots by night in some of Tiger Bay's lowest dives: here he'd be roistering with his deep-bosom harpies till the crows of dawn.

Well, Bridget had been married to Caesar for about three years, I suppose, when I saw her outside my Presbytery coming in her pony and trap.

"Good mornin', Sean O'Brien!" cried she. "A foine summer day it is to be sure," and her voice was as gentle as the summer Connemara wind.

The sun was like bottled glass, I remember, the distant hills like hot loaves straight from the baker's dozen. "How're ye doin', Bridget Mary?" I bawled, and came nearer, and I saw in her face the beauty she was before her death in the arms of Correlli.

"Ach, not so bad," she replied. "But I'm lonely for me little Johnny who's over with the good nuns at Nazareth House, for Caesar won't have him up at Radyr, as ye know."

"We all make mistakes, girl, and Caesar's making his, according to reports. Can't you persuade him to treat the boy as his own?" and she replied, stepping down from the trap,

"Don't judge the generosity of other men by yourself, Sean O'Brien," and with this she glanced up, crying in mock fear, "Look out, look out, we're about to be run over."

"Run for it, run for it!" I shouted, picking up my skirts. "It's the Charabanc Outing!"

Whooping and hurrahing about fifty kids came racing over the Bobtail towards us. Mostly barefooted, they came in rags with Minnie Ha Ha and her brood of six brothers, Butch aged four, Randy and Kiernen, the twins, Topsy and Pat, Alfie and his lot from Pendoylan and Poll, aged two, who had wet her drawers. Reaching us they linked hands and used us as maypoles, dancing around us.

"Ach, Mrs. Correlli, will ye hand the Priest a shillin' for the Outing?"

"Or a sixpence so he can buy us your chap's ice-creams?"

"Will ye be coming, too? There's room, lady."

"Father O'Brien, Father O'Brien, will ye sit me on the pony?"

Melissa, whose father had been lost at sea, knelt at Bridget's feet, so we opened our pockets and handed out pennies, with me scolding and hauling them back for not thanking properly.

"The Charabanc Outing?" asked Bridget, after the children had gone.

"An annual bun fight down at Barry — Jim Driscoll and the mothers help. Now we've started it we can't stop it."

"All your children, eh, Sean?" she said, her eyes wistful. "Father to a hundred and a parent to none?"

"That's the size of it." I gave her a grin.

"Dear God," said she. "What a fool I've been. I'd have done better to share the poverty of a good man like you on the rocks of

Ballacroy, than enjoy a whore's wealth in the city with Caesar Correlli..."

"Don't talk like that!" I whispered.

"For aren't I the same as his harlots, except that I've me marriage lines to make it legal?"

Unaccountably, I put my arms about her, and such was the sudden radiance of her face that I thought Jesus might have touched her; and she was soft and warm against me so that I remembered again our youth in Connemara.

"I'd best be going," said Bridget Mary, with business, and she did.

"All right, all right, what's going on?" asked God, when she'd got clear.

"Nothing," I said, giving him an eye at the sun.

"Look," said he. "I've never handed out licences for my priests to spark in broad daylight, and I'm not starting now."

"She's an old friend!" I retorted. "What do you expect of us down here?"

"More than I'm getting," replied God. "That woman's made her bed and she's got to lie on it; I'm not having you in beside her, understand? Besides, she's Caesar's wife and should be beyond reproach, so don't let me catch you with your cassock up, O'Brien. She's in trouble enough — better priests than you have been unfrocked for less than public devotions. Are you listening?"

"You're a hard man at times, so ye are."

"You can say that again," said God.

Now later still, about the beginning of September, rooks were boasting to the sun about Wales; white pot-bellied monks were lumbering across the sky of blue — St. Peter beginning his weekly wash — and up came Bridget Mary behind me.

"Will you confess me, holy man?" asked she.

So we went into the Confessional and I bent my thick ear to the holy grille.

"I've come to confess that I'm in love with you, Sean O'Brien," said Bridget.

I thought my hearing had gone wrong, but she said, "Years ago I could have had you back in Ballacroy before you were ordained..."

"Should you be telling me this?" I asked.

"She should not," said God, but only I heard him, apparently, for she continued:

"Listen, Sean. I've just bought a white cottage on the shores of Ballacroy. I've tasted the soil and water, and they're good and clean, like the love I'm offerin' you. For aren't you as sick to death of the poverty and tide-swill of this place. Oh, Sean O'Brien, didn't you care for me well a long time ago? Or will ye say I was anybody's girl back home and Caesar's wife back here? Do you not remember the nights along the strand of Ballacroy, when we walked under the stars? Listen, I'm leaving this place and going home — I'm leaving all the wealth and the dirt of it all, and I'm leaving the man who doesn't give a jot for me. Give me the chance I missed before, Sean. For I'd wash your clothes and cook and mend for you; I'd keep my body fair, and I darn like a new pin. Listen, I could even give you a son."

She had broken me, and I bowed my head and called her name, which was not her name but the one by which I knew her. "Oh, Macushla, Macushla, do not make it harder than it is for me," and she put a finger through the holy grille and touched my hand, and the touch, I tell ye, was like a burn, and she said:

"You left me in Ballycroy for the God we love. But would he not understand if you left him now, for me? Jesus, Mary and Joseph, he's had you for the past five years!" and I opened my eyes upon her and saw that she was weeping.

Back in my Presbytery now, I clasped my hands and knelt before His Cross.

"Upon my soul," said God, when I put the problem to him, "you do get us both into the most impossible situations. Look, son, leave it for a fortnight or so, for I've a rebellion in Chile, a convocation in Nice, some accounts at the Vatican I've got to square up, and there's a fella in a dog collar walking round naked in a barrel at a place called Stiffkey. Who is this woman you're on about? Do I know her?"

"Her name's Bridget Mary O'Callaghan — I told you before, Your Honour. Your memory's goin' again."

"O aye. Do you love her?"

"From the moment I saw her."

"And her little lad's yours, did you say?"

"He is not mine, and I didn't say so!" I retorted.

"All right, all right, keep your hair on," said God. "I'll put a B/F on this one and come back to you when I can. And O'Brien..."

"Yes, Sir."

"Do try not to get so involved, especially with the women."

I bowed to him.

Well, for the next few nights I tossed and turned in nightmare dreams of indecision, seeing visions of Tiger Bay in all its stinks and poverty; the cruelty of the rich, the disregard of the poor — the skimping and scraping, the drunken brawls; but I saw, also, the marvellous sacrifices of parents struggling to keep decent; the fine dignity of men like Jim Driscoll, who had given his all for the people of Irishtown. But a white cottage by the shores of the Atlantic beckoned me with undying force; the red lips of Bridget Mary called me and I held her softness against me in the arms of my man's mind. And at dawn on the last day of September, with the rooks shouting their nuts off in the trees of the Bobtail, I got up, washed, shaved and shampooed and got myself ready for whatever the day might bring; and sure enough, I found a letter from my darling girl lying on the hall mat.

With fumbling fingers I tore open the envelope, and read:

'Shore Cottage, Ballacroy,
Connemara, Ireland.

Dearest one,

I'm here by the fire writing this, with our son asleep beside me. Yes, your son, Sean O'Brien. For how could I tell you he was yours with you about to be married to the Church? Forgive me, and may the God we both love make the choice.

Macushla.'

That settled it. I went back into the bedroom and packed my suitcase. For there had grown within me a delight that filled me with a new sense of purpose. A son. *A son*. He was mine. Johnny of the bright hair, a miniature man. I was renewed, reborn, for a man without a son is but a meteor flashing across the sky. I thought: We would go together in the quiet places hand in hand. On the sands of Ballacroy we would walk, my son and me. I would tell him of the Great Places beyond the sea, of fair lands, of men and women of the deserts made fertile, where the men are seven feet tall and the women have glorious breasts and the carriage of queens. And I would build in my son the strength and goodness of the man I might have been before I wilted to the onslaught of the world. How beautiful he would be, my son; moulded to perfection by his mother's pain!

Hauling my suitcase through the hall, I got as far as the front door when I heard the voice.

"I'm back," said God.

I swung about, my arms held wide. "I've got a son. Did ye hear that? The woman's just told me — I've got a son."

"That's what I suggested, but you bit my head off," said God.

"Did you think I haven't known it all these years?"

I began to tremble. The trembling crept to my hands and I fought to control it, saying, "Now I know he's mine, I... I'll have to go. Please, please don't stop me now," and I lifted the suitcase.

"Ach, that's furthest from my intentions," replied God. "It won't be the first time a priest has walked out on the job, and it won't be the last, I suppose. But have ye stopped to consider you'll be living in sin? She's not asking you over to Ballacroy for steamed pudding and cream puffs, for all she's a cook'..

It stilled me, and I lowered the suitcase, and God continued, "Well, actually, you won't be staining your soul because Caesar Correlli's just shot himself — no, don't took at me like that, I had no hand in it. He was out killing my small creatures and fell on his gun. So the coast is clear, O'Brien, your conscience and all."

I gripped my hands, whispering, "I'm obliged to you, and I'll never forget this, Your Honour."

"Mind you," said God, "there's only one thing bothering me now. It's a case of balancing one thing against another, I suppose. You see, you've only got one son over at Ballacroy, but you've got about ten thousand here."

I closed my eyes, and He added, "Up to you, mind. You've always been a good priest — you're due for promotion up here, I can tell you — and I'll tell you one thing more. Whatever you decide the God of love goes with you," and with that the hall door came open.

The hall door came open and the September sun flooded in. And I saw beyond the Bobtail the waiting charabanc and about fifty ragged urchins piling across the grass towards me. Like the dregs of the French Revolution they came, waving their banners and sticks, already stuck up with toffee apples and sherbert dabs, for Jim Driscoll and the Nazareth nuns were among them. Minnie Ha Ha was shrieking with delight; Topsy and Randy, Kiernen and Paul, Willie and Kath, Sam and Mavoureen — all were there — with Poll waving a stick of Tiger rock and holding up her drawers. And up to the Presbytery door they came, jigging and jogging around me, pulling at my clothes.

"Father O'Brien! Father O'Brien! Father O'Brien!"

"Mr. Driscoll's got your sandwiches!"

"Do you think it's going to rain?"

"Are ye ready?"

"Are you comin'?"

"I've got his suitcase," said Butch, dragging it towards the charabanc.

I wiped my mouth with the back of my hand. "Aye, I'm coming," I said, and looked up at the sun, whispering, "Dear God. You certainly know how to handle folks, don't you?"

"I ought to," answered God. "I've been at it long enough."

• • •

Obituary

'Her eyes were black and shadowed heavy in her highboned face; black was her hair and tied with red ribbon, and it reached to her waist. Her dress was red, her petticoats yellow, and around her head was a band of scarlet.'

• 12 •

Obituary

I was just settling for an afternoon nap when a big hefty wench comes knocking on the Presbytery door.

"Father," said Martha, me old housekeeper, coming in, "there's a fine big wench in the hall saying she's come to live with you."

"Is that a fact?" said I. "Is she aware I'm nearing senile decay?"

"I told her that," said Martha, "but she doesn't care if you're nine or ninety."

"Show her in."

"Is that wise?"

"Show her in," I said.

It was the spring of 1919 and the lads were still coming home from the war. All the wives up and down the Newtown street were giving each other bits of their minds and scrubbing their little semicircles of purity into the world. And since there was a nip in the air I called into the *Duke of Edinburgh* for a glass for medicinal purposes, for Jim Driscoll, the boxer landlord, didn't reckon to take holy money.

"Is the new relative settling in, Father?" he asked me.

"Ach," I replied, "She's fair and beautiful, and I'd have it no different, but she's not a relative."

"So it's true, is it? And do you realise the parish tongues are wagging, holy man?"

"My son, while they're scandalising me, they're not doin' anyone else."

I sank me whisky and he totted me another. Jim said, "Listen, I'd knock the heads together of any two men in the world if I hear them gabbling, but you realise you could finish up in front o' the Pope?"

"Don't remind me."

"And is it true old Martha's taken off?"

"Two women in one kitchen, lad, you know what women are."

"God preserve us," said Jim.

Well, I did me rounds and finished up with Mrs. Ten Beynon, who was having an assisted delivery up in Pendolyan: then I went home and found the new lodger in the kitchen sitting in Martha's chair with her high-buttoned boots up on the table, and she had a fair leg on her, let me tell ye. My stomach was growling like pounce thunder, for I hadn't eaten properly in the week since Martha left. But, mind you, there were compensations: even a cleric is entitled to beauty, and this one wasn't behind the door when looks were handed out.

"Good morning, holy Father!" cried she, and she looked like Delilah must have done before she put the screws on Ahab.

Listen!

Her eyes were black and shadowed heavy in her highboned face; black was her hair and tied with red ribbon, and it reached to her waist. Her dress was red, her petticoats yellow, and around her head was a band of scarlet.

"Bridget Eve O'Hallorhan," I said, "It's been lovely having you, but my life's turned upside down, and you'll have me up in front of the Bishop. What's more, you can't cook like Martha now, can ye?"

"Ach no, sweet man!" cried she. "But I thought you liked my

spotted dick?"

"Your spotted dick, woman, is one worse than your steak and kidney, and that's uneatable. Will you find your way out in the manner you came in?" and she got to her feet and went pert and sad, nearly bringing the tears to my eyes, and said:

"Would you send me away, and you a man of God? After all, I am your responsibility, aren't I?"

"My responsibility? Are you looney?"

"Ach, sure, Father! For didn't you register me birth twenty-one years ago in County Wexford, and christened me Bridget Eve O'Hallorhan?"

"Even if I did, what right have you to plant yourself on a celibate priest and begin to starve him to death? In the name of pity, leave me in peace and I'll bring back Martha, who's a cook."

This burst her into tears, and I had my arms around her when a letter came through the door.

It was from the Bishop.

"Father O'Brien," said the Bishop, after I'd kissed the ring, "can you expect me to condone you living with a scarlet woman? True, old Martha was no great shakes on a leg parade, man, but you're going to a bag of bones, and the parish is scandalised. This Bridget Eve O'Hallorhan, for all she's got a wicked eye and a fine thigh on her, will have to go in the name of your constitution. And what makes her think she's got a call on you?"

"Because I christened her and registered her birth."

Said his Lordship, "Now that's true because I've checked with County Wexford, but do you realise that Bridget Eve O'Hallorhan doesn't exist at all? Because she died, the sweet infant, two days after you registered her birth ..." And he went pompous and straightened up and made no eyes to mention. "I suggest you go home and have a real good look at the person you call Bridget Eve O'Hallorhan, the interloper you exchanged for Martha, your cook."

So this I did, and found Bridget in the kitchen burning a roast to a cinder and putting sugar in the gravy.

But how to describe the beauty of her, with only words to use?

"Good evening, holy Father," said she. "Have you been having it out with the Pope? And did he agree to me staying?"

"Ye sweet darlin'," I answered, and came nearer and looked into her face. And I saw in her, for the first time, a strange and awful radiance; and I felt, standing before her, that I was in the presence of sanctity, something of the Divine, yet infernal: banshees and bawdies I heard, a satanic torment of ghouls sighing between demons and celestial bliss.

It was her eyes.

"Ach, ye dear earthly thing," said she, and her arms went about me. "I want to stay wi' me darlin' Priest."

"No, girl, you'll have to go," I said, levering her off, and left her and went into the library and took up a pen and paper, and wrote:

'To: The Daily Express.
Obituary Column.

Kindly publish the following:

'Bridget Eve O'Hallorhan. Born 20th May 1898 in County Wexford. Died in infancy. Rest her soul in peace.'

Next Tuesday when the obituary notice was published, Bridget disappeared and Martha returned.

"You poor fella," said Martha, patting my ribs. "She starved ye, so she did — you're nothin' but a bag o' bones."

But they only eat manna in Heaven, and when the great call comes and I answer Gabriel's Horn, Bridget Eve O'Hallorhan will have more to offer than Martha, for there's more to a woman than cooking — there's looking, as is widely known.

• • •

O'Brien's Christmas Ghost

'...a week before Christmas, it was — poor Shaun was drowned in Cardiff Bay. And all Eileen had to show he had ever existed was a sovereign in her tea-caddy, a child in her womb and around her neck a tiny fish-bone crucifix.'

• 13 •

O'Brien's Christmas Ghost

From my Presbytery near St. Paul's I used to watch me parishioners' activities, like the off-shift dockers playing pitch and toss; who was coming out of the *Green Fields of Erin* without a leg under him, and who got her eye filled up a week last Sunday.

I was right keen on marital activites, ye see, so kept an eye on skirts in the dark. Therefore, it sparked me interest when young Shaun and Eileen started goin' mooney, with down from feather mattresses blowing up between them.

Young Shaun had come on since he signed as a deck-hand on the *Neale and West* fishing trawlers on Bute Dock East, and wee Eileen was trembling and expectant, which was under-standable.

The pair of 'em used to go to the Park Hall flicks most Saturday nights — ach, dear me, it was a joy to see them all — the lasses all curled up or shingled and the lads smelling of bay rum after-shave and their waves put in with condensed milk.

And they'd sit in the back stalls, this lot, the chaps with eyes like constipated owls and the girls with their noses stuck up into the Nestles, and stop-its and pleases were the order of the night.

Well, to cut an Irish yarn short, I married Shaun and Eileen — I couldn't get them to the altar fast enough — and they set up house in 3 Pendoylan Place, not far from where Jim Driscoll, the boxer, used to live.

But, a fortnight or so after the wedding — a week before Christmas, it was — poor Shaun was drowned in Cardiff Bay.

And all Eileen had to show he had ever existed was a sovereign in her tea-caddy, a child in her womb, and around her neck a tiny fish-bone crucifix taken from the body of a ballan wrasse, which, as everyone knows, is a holy fish: inscribed on its little silver mounting were the words, "I will come back to you," and this Eileen wore in the divide of her breast.

"The ballan wrasse crucifix was put there by God," said Eileen, bitterly, "but it didn't do a lot to protect my Shaun!"

"Don't talk like that, sweet girl," I said to her, and I knelt beside her in the kitchen of 3 Pendoylan, and she raised her tear-stained face to the moonlit window, and cried:

"Now prove you're God! Do ye job and send him home to me!"

I held her and she wept, and would not be comforted.

Now, a day or two later I was in the tap-room of the *Duke of Edinburgh*, sinking a quart and lecturing the customers on the evils of strong drink, when in comes a drunk at a rush, crying, "Father O'Brien, Father O'Brien! There's a skeleton in rags with seaweed on its feet, hammerin' at the door of Eileen Devlin's place!"

"Is that a fact," I said. "Then run back and give him the compliments of the season," and I was just killing my glass when Jobey Downs, the Connemara undertaker, slides up and whispers into me ear:

"But, there's somethin' queer going' on, nevertheless, holy Father, for I saw him meself last night. I swear to God I saw him; young Shaun Devlin with a halo round his head, letting himself into his widow's No.3."

"What's wrong wi' that?" I demanded. "He lives there, doesn't he?"

"Ay ay, sure enough, but the fella's supposed to be dead, or don't you remember? We put him down, the sod."

"You mind your language in front of the Cloth," says I.

For the next couple of days, however, I kept an eye on young Eileen Devlin, since the chance might arise for a bit of exorcising, and sightings of Shaun Devlin in various guises continued to come in.

His visits to Eileen, I discovered, coincided with the return to port of his *Neale and West* trawler. The fella, I decided, was behaving in the most irresponsible manner, and I got the proof of this when I met his Eileen in Ellen Street by the Bobtail.

And she was no longer the wailing young hag at the funeral, let me tell ye; she was dressed in scarlet with a boa round her neck, looking as cheerful as a young bride and twice as healthy.

"Ach, ye darlin' thing, Father O'Brien," she cries, and gives me a wink. "Me prayers have been answered at last, so they have — that ballan wrasse crucifix worked after all — I've got me chap back in me bed."

"Have ye indeed!" says I.

"And he's as fit as a little flea, let me tell ye!" and she laughed into the winter sun as if contained by some queer madness.

"Is he now?" I answered. "Would he be strong enough to have a word or two with me in private, do ye think?"

"Ach for sure!" She smiled into my face and made no eyes to speak of. "Look, he's due back in port on Christmas Eve — tomorrow. Would early evening suit you, Father — in 3 Pendoylan?"

"I'll be there," I replied, and the moment she'd turned up Tyndall Street I realised that I couldn't be there at all, because next morning I'd be sailing for County Wexford, to spend Christmas with my own people. "Mrs. Devlin!" I called. "Mrs. Devlin!" But she didn't hear me, I suppose.

But the steamer I took next day never reached Wexford, for it sank in a storm in Cardiff Bay, and it was lucky that the lifeboat took us off or many would be having watery graves. So I found myself back in Newtown wetter than I'd been in all my life, but able to visit the Devlins after all, God be praised.

I noticed, by chance, as I came off the lifeboat in Bute Dock East, that the *Neale and West* trawlers hadn't come in yet —

delayed, I suppose, by the same freak storm.

That evening, I washed and changed and went over to 3 Pendoylan, and the Devlin house; a bit late, aye, for darkness was over the earth. Young Eileen didn't answer my knock, so I climbed the stairs to her room since she wasn't in the kitchen.

Standing by her bedside, I watched Eileen in sleep.

Being a celibate, I know not the secrets of women, but that ballan wrasse crucifix, I thought, was privileged indeed to lie in the shadowed divide of her breast ... and I closed my eyes and envied Shaun, her man.

And then I heard the street door come open and shut, and so did Eileen; I drew deeper into the shadows of the room as she sat up in the bed. So beautiful she looked, with her eyes bright and her lips parted in expectancy as the bedroom door opened and Shaun came in.

"Shaun!" And she opened her arms to him like a wife. "Oh Shaun!"

But he saw me first, despite the darkness. "Why Holy Father!" he cried. "You're here with us, you're here with us, God be praised!" and he wrung my hands in greeting.

"Don't waste time on us," I said, pushing him away. "We've a perpetual Heaven in which to talk — see to the mortal first, son, look, she's dyin' for you, and we're both dead, see to your girl."

And he knelt by the bed and covered her face with kisses.

ALSO PUBLISHED BY BLORENGE BOOKS

CORDELL COUNTRY
by Chris Barber.

Inspired by Alexander Cordell's moving novel *Rape of the Fair Country*, Chris Barber set out to write a walker's guide to locations featured in the novel. The result is a historical walking guide flavoured with quotations from Cordell's novel and the writings of early 19th century visitors to Blaenafon and Nantyglo where the action of the novel takes place. Six circular walks from convenient starting points are described. They take in the Blorenge hill which looms dramatically over Abergavenny and visit industrial features such as Llanfoist Wharf and inclines, Hill's Tramroad, Garnddyrys Forge and Rolling Mill site, Pwll-du tunnel and quarry and Blaenafon Ironworks. A walk is also provided near the fortified round towers of Crawshay Bailey (the 19th century ironmaster) at Nantyglo and the final route crosses the moorland of Mynydd Llangynidr in search of the remote and elusive Chartists' Cave.

The book is profusely illustrated with line drawings and maps specially prepared by local artist Michael Blackmore who has brought to life scenes from the past — recreating industrial life in the 19th century which has been so vividly described by Cordell in his novel.

ISBN 0 9510444 00 £4.20

STONE AND STEAM IN THE BLACK MOUNTAINS
by David Tipper.

The remote unspoiled uplands of the Black Mountains were once invaded by hundreds of navvies, stonemasons and craftsmen whose job it was to construct the isolated Grwyne Fawr Reservoir. They built, blasted, boozed and brawled their way through a seemingly impossible task which, instead of the estimated 40 months, took no less than 18 years to complete. The work required the creation of a mountain village for over 400 people with a 12 mile railway line which climbed to 1800 ft.

His 40 year acquaintance with the Welsh Border has brought the Rev. Tipper into personal contact with many families who worked for the former Abertillery and District Water Works and he tells the story of this early 20th century struggle with vivid clarity and compelling interest.

ISBN 0 9510444 1 9 £3.90

THE ROMANCE OF THE WELSH MOUNTAINS
by Chris Barber.

Covering the mountains of Wales from Snowdonia to the Brecon Beacons, this anthology has been compiled by Chris Barber who is well known as the author of several books on Wales. He has a wide experience of walking and climbing in the Welsh mountains and this book is illustrated with a selection of his own photographs that capture the atmosphere so special to this part of the British Isles.

His aim has been to present a picture of the days when the first cragsmen and walkers in Wales had 'opportunities for pioneering routes in places where no man had moved before, in those times when solitude can be found on the Snowdonia summits even on a hot summer day.'

It is in fact a literary journey through the mountains of Wales and will appeal to the hill walker, scrambler or rock climber, and all those who love wild places. It is ideal for reading in the hut, the hostel or the hotel. Campers may delve into it whilst waiting for the stew to simmer, or the pub to open, or more than likely the rain to stop. Alternatively it may be enjoyed by the armchair reader sitting at home by the fireside dreaming of those mountains far away.

ISBN 0 9510444 2 7 £4.50